William

Just—William a facsimile of the first (1922) edition
The William Companion by Mary Cadogan
The Woman Behind William: a life of Richmal Crompton
by Mary Cadogan
Just William's World—a pictorial map
by Gillian Clements and Kenneth Waller
School is a Waste of Time!
by William Brown (and Richmal Crompton)

MR. MONSON'S FACE WAS CONGESTED WITH ANGER.

William
the Superman

RICHMAL CROMPTON

Illustrated by Henry Ford

M

MACMILLAN CHILDREN'S BOOKS

First published 1968

© Richmal Crompton Lamburn 1968

Illustrations by Henry Ford
copyright © Pan Macmillan Children's Books

First published in this edition 1993 by
PAN MACMILLAN CHILDREN'S BOOKS
A division of Pan Macmillan Limited
London and Basingstoke
Associated companies throughout the world.

1 3 5 7 9 8 6 4 2

ISBN 0–333–58606–9

A CIP catalogue record for this book is available from
the British Library

Phototypeset by Intype, London

Printed and bound in Great Britain by
Cox & Wyman Ltd, Reading

Contents

William invites you!

Join my club and becum a nOutlaw
William Brown

You can join the new Outlaws Club!

You will receive
✳a special Outlaws wallet containing
the new Outlaws badge
the club rules and membership card
a pad for secret messages
a club pencil
and
a letter from William giving you the secret password

Chapter 1

William and the New Civilisation

"It was a jolly good story," said Henry. "It was in a book my father got out of the library an' I read it while I was at home with that cold."

"What was it about?" said William.

"It was about an atom bomb war," said Henry, "an' only four people were left alive at the end an' they had to start a new civ'lisation."

"Gosh! I'd like to do that," said William. "I could make a jolly sight better one than the one we've got now."

"It takes years to make a civ'lisation," said Ginger.

"It needn't, said William. "I bet I could make one jolly quick. It'd be like goin' back to prehistoric times an' startin' all over again. I've always wanted to do that. I've seen pictures of prehistoric times an' they look smashin'."

"I've seen pictures of 'em, too," said Douglas. "They look jolly dangerous to me."

The Outlaws had been driven into the old barn by a heavy shower of rain and were carrying on a desultory conversation while they waited for the sudden downpour to cease.

Jumble sat in the doorway, watching the downpour and thumping his tail on the ground occasionally, as if in approval of what one or another of the boys was saying.

"It's not a bit dangerous," said William. "It's modern civ'lisation that's dangerous with all these motor-cars an'—an' escaped crim'nals an'—an' people puttin' hedges an' fences round int'restin' places so's you've got to scrape through them or climb over them an'—an' homework wearin' people's brains out—it's all that that's dangerous . . . Come on! Let's think what we'd do if we had to start civ'lisation all over again."

"It's stoppin' rainin'," said Douglas.

"No, it isn't," said Ginger. "It's comin' on harder than ever. Anyway it's no use thinkin' what you'd do to start another civ'lisation after an atom bomb war 'cause it's not likely to happen."

"It *could* happen," said Henry slowly. "That's what this book was about. It could happen quite easily an' quite suddenly. Someone in some country's only got to get mad an' press a button an' the whole thing's over in no time an'—an'—well, p'raps jus' four people left alive to start a new civ'lisation."

"Same as us four," said Ginger.

"Yes, an' it might *be* us four," said William. "I mean, there's no reason why it shouldn't be us four as well as anyone else's four."

"An' it might all happen in a second," said Henry.

"Well, then we ought to be makin' some sort of preparations," said William. "No good leavin' it to the last minute. If we're goin' to be the only four left alive in the world to start a new civ'lisation, we ought to be thinkin' it out."

"What is there to think out?" said Ginger.

"Gosh, there's *lots*," said William. "We've got to think what sort of civ'lisation we're goin' to have."

"Y-yes," said Henry. "There's education to start with . . ."

"We won't bother about that," said William. "I've had education all my life an' I don't see it's done me any good. I often think I'd have been better off without it."

"Readin' an' writin's useful," said Henry.

"Yes, we could have a bit of them," said William, "but we don't want geography or French or hist'ry or any of that sort of thing, 'cause there won't *be* any of them. I mean, the whole world'll be wiped out except us."

"It'll be like after the flood in the Bible," said Douglas.

"What about food?" said Ginger.

"Savages live on berries," said Henry.

"I once tried doin' that an' it made me sick," said Douglas.

"Prehistoric people lived on wild animals," said William, "an' we're goin' back to bein' prehistoric . . . We'll need wild animals' skins to dress in, too."

"There won't *be* any wild animals," said Ginger. "They'll all have got wiped out by this atom bomb."

"There might be a few left in the Zoo or somewhere," said William. "Stands to reason. If a few yumans get left a few animals might, too."

"They'd be tame ones if they came out of the Zoo," said Henry. "Nearly all Zoo animals are tame."

"Well, we could start with 'em tame an' train 'em up to be wild," said William. "We'd better start with quite small ones. There's Henry's mouse . . ."

"You'd never make him wild," said Henry, "an' he's too small, anyway."

"Well, everything was small to start with," said Ginger, "then this thing called evolution came along an' made 'em big."

"That took *years*," said William, "an' we can't wait for years. We're eleven already. There's not all that much of our lives left. An' this atom bomb might go off any minute."

"An' I bet wild animals are jolly hard to cook," said Ginger. "We couldn't eat 'em raw."

"Tins would be safer," said Douglas.

"All right, we'll bring a few tins," said William.

"Prehistoric people started growin' corn for food," said Henry.

"I 'spect that's what they did after the flood, too," said Douglas. "I could get some corn to sow. Miss Polliter, next door, keeps hens an' she keeps the corn she feeds 'em on in her shed. I could easy get a bit an' we'll sow it for food."

"That'll be all right," said William. "An' we've fixed on not havin' any schools."

"People ought to know a bit of arithmetic," said Henry, "so's they can count."

"Gosh, we can count without arithmetic," said William. "We've got fingers, haven't we?"

"What about books?" said Ginger.

"Well, p'raps jus' one book," said William. "But they're not necess'ry. I can't think of a single book that need've got printed. P'raps jus' one book so's this new civ'lisation'll be able to spell things like 'Keep Out' when they've got sep'rate bits of land to live on."

"What about houses?" said Henry.

"Oh, we won't have *houses*," said William. "Gosh, no! Not houses with carpets an' ornaments an' furniture an' stuff. That's one of the things that's wrong with civ'lis-ation. We'll have native huts."

"It'll be *jus'* the same as after the flood," said Douglas. The reflection seemed to give him confidence and satisfaction. "I bet they made native huts then."

"What'll we make 'em of?" said Ginger.

"Oh, cut down trees an' things," said William, vaguely.

"We'll need tools," said Ginger.

"Yes," said William. "That's one of the things we'll have to c'lect. We ought to start c'lecting things now. I mean, if it's all goin' to be over as quick as Henry says we ought to have things ready."

"Where shall we keep the things?" said Ginger.

William looked all round the dim recesses of the old barn.

"This is a jolly good place," he said. "We could bring the things here an' keep 'em here. We could cover 'em up with sacks an' stuff. No one'd notice them. No one comes here but us, anyway . . . We'll bring the things on Saturday. Douglas can bring the corn an' the rest of us anything we think'll be useful an' we'll sort 'em out when we've c'lected them . . . It's time to go home to lunch now. I'm jolly hungry an' it's shepherd's pie."

"You'll have to get used to berries," said Ginger.

"I will all right when the time comes," said William.

"They could have fish in the ark," said Douglas.

William was the first to arrive. He brought a saw with wildly uneven teeth, a broom-handle and a watering-can with a gaping hole in one side. A tin opener protruded from one pocket, a torch from the other, and an old motor-tyre hung round his neck. Ginger arrived shortly afterwards. He carried a tennis racquet with several strings missing, a pair of roller skates, a boxing-glove and a tin of baked beans. They threw critical glances at each other's contributions as they ranged them in a corner of the old barn.

"I bet we can straighten out the saw," said William, "an' the broom-handle makes a jolly good club. Pre-historic people always had clubs."

"What about the tyre?" said Ginger.

"We could do *lots* of things with that," said William.
"I found it in the ditch near our house and it seemed a
pity to let it go. You can see it's been a good one. I bet
it'll come in useful. We could build a sort of vehicle round
it or—we could mend that hole in the watering-can with
it—you do mend things with rubber—an' then it would
do for carryin' things, an' look!"—he dived into his pocket
and brought out a box of matches—"I've brought these
to start a fire with. We'll need fire in this new
civ'lisation. . . . What've you brought that tennis racquet
for? There's not much of it left."

"It'd make a good weapon," said Ginger. "It's jolly
strong. An' we could use it for lots of things."

"One boxin' glove isn't much use," said William.

"Yes, it is," said Ginger. "It's better than none,
anyway."

"What about the sieve?"

"Well, I though that if we had to drink water from the
river we could strain it through the sieve to keep the
germs out."

"A new civ'lisation can't be fussy about germs," said
William. "I bet those prehistoric people didn't worry
about germs." He examined the sieve more closely.
"There's a lot of holes missin'. I bet hundreds of germs
could get through."

"Well, it's an old one they'd thrown away," said
Ginger. "I couldn't have got it if they hadn't. An' I
thought the roller skates'd be jolly useful. There won't be
any wild horses to tame an' it'll be *years* before we can
invent trains an' we may have to travel long distances in
this new civ'lisation . . . Here's Henry. I bet he's brought
some good stuff."

Henry's contributions, however, were a little disappointing. He had felt responsible for the artistic and literary culture of the new civilisation and had brought with him an ancient, battered brief-case, from which he drew a London Telephone Directory for 1958 and a much foxed engraving of a portrait of Mr. Gladstone. His only concessions to the practical side of the situation were a billycan and a ball of string.

"What on earth have you brought those for?" said William, pointing to the telephone directory and the engraving of Mr. Gladstone.

"Well, I thought we ought to have a *bit* of education," said Henry apologetically. "There's *heaps* of words in the telephone directory. They'd teach anyone spellin' that wanted to learn. An' there's some geography, too. There's a map of all the places round London. It might come in useful."

"And what about *him*?" said William, looking with disfavour at the rugged features of Mr. Gladstone.

The note of apology in Henry's voice deepened.

"It's been stuck up in the loft with a lot of rubbish for years," he said, "but it's a *picture*. It's *art*. Someone must have *drawn* it. I thought it was better than nothin' to start off this civ'lisation on art when it's ready for it. . . . I've been thinkin' about music, too. We ought to give this new civ'lisation a bit of music." He drew a trumpet from the depth of the brief-case. "I thought this'd be better than nothin'. I had it when I was a herald in the school play."

William looked at it with qualified approval.

"Well, I s'pose it makes a *noise*," he said, "an' that's all music is when you come to think of it. Yes, it might be useful . . . Wonder where Douglas is. He was bringin' the seeds an' they're jolly important."

Douglas could be seen making his way slowly across the field. He trundled a one-legged wheelbarrow that

DOUGLAS COULD BE SEEN MAKING HIS WAY SLOWLY ACROSS
THE FIELD.

seemed to contain a weird assortment of all sorts of mis-
cellaneous goods.

"I don't see that these are goin' to be much use,"
said Ginger, turning over the contents. "An ole lamp
shade . . . lace mats . . . a spectacle-case, empty . . . an
ole hat . . . Gosh! *Look* at it . . . toasting-fork . . . a box
of buttons . . ."

"Well, I got them out of the bag where my mother
keeps things for the jumble sales," explained Douglas.
"She'd gone in the garden an' I had to get what I could
as quick as I could, before she came back. It's all stuff
she doesn't want an' I thought it'd be more useful in this
new civ'lisation than mendin' the roof of the Village Hall

which is all these jumble sales are for an' it always starts leakin' again in time for the next."

"But *listen*," broke in William. "You were goin' to bring *seeds*. Corn seeds to get crops growin' for food."

"Yes, I know," said Douglas guiltily. "I did try. I went round to the shed where Miss Polliter keeps the corn an' she'd gone away for the day an' the shed was locked up. I couldn't get in so I couldn't get this corn, but my fam'ly had tinned corn for lunch an' didn't eat much of it so I took what was left out of the fridge an' put it in a plastic bag to bring. I thought it would be all right. It's *corn*. I thought it might *grow*."

"Well, where is it?" said William.

Douglas's eyes slid away from William's.

"I—I sort of jus' tasted it on the way," he said. "Jus' to make sure it tasted all right, an' it did taste all right, an' I was a bit hungry an'—an——"

"You *ate* it," said William sternly.

"I didn't mean to," protested Douglas. "I didn't know I had done till I had done . . . but—" he burrowed in the wheelbarrow—"I've brought a cabbage. I pinched it out of the garden. I thought it would stop us gettin' scurvy."

"*Look!*" said Ginger, who was standing in the doorway. "Gosh! Look who's comin'."

They joined him in the doorway. A straggling procession of children was coming across the field towards the old barn. They were children from the village, all well known to the Outlaws.

The holidays were nearing their end, and the children, having exhausted their possibilities, lawful and unlawful, were feeling bored and frustrated. They had now reached the point when any diversion was better than none. Then the news had spread. . . . Douglas, never very good at keeping a secret, had dropped vague and ambiguous hints. Ginger, though he had answered no questions, had worn a tantalising air of secret knowledge. William's brow was furrowed; his face wore the expression of one who is making momentous decisions, carrying weighty responsibilities. Suspicion became a certainty. Something was afoot and William Brown, as usual, was leader and organiser. Their spirits rose. With William in command, things could be counted on to move quickly, unpredictably, into mysterious realms of danger, hazard, drama and adventure. Rumour followed rumour. Ella Poppleham was convinced that the end of the world was coming and that William had advance knowledge of the date and was making his preparations. Freddie Parker, whose form was 'doing' *Richard the Second* at school, thought that the mysterious Event was to be something on the lines of the Peasants' Revolt, while Jimmy Barlow, whose father was the President of the local Conservative Association, insisted that it would turn out to be a surprise General Election. But it was Douglas's guarded hints, growing less guarded as his questioners pressed him more closely, that seemed to solve the mystery.

"It's another flood," said Ella Poppleham, "an' William Brown's the only one that knows when it's comin'."

"Yes, William Brown *would*," said Arabella Simpkin with a sniff. Arabella always tried to conceal her secret respect for William under a show of contempt. " 'E'd find out anythin' anywhere, would William Brown. Pokin' 'is nose in where it isn't wanted. Even in floods. Doesn't care 'oo gets drowned as long as it's not 'im. Well, 'e can *'ave* 'is ole flood for all I care."

But they kept a watchful eye on the Outlaws and their doings, and, when they saw them carrying their belongings across the field to the old barn, there seemed to be no room for further doubt. The flood was due to begin and the Outlaws were preparing some sort of ark in the old barn. They might even have made an ark somewhere else and were assembling essential supplies in the old barn. However that might be, the children were decided on one point. They were not going to be left out of it. Their boredom and dejection vanished. Swiftly, furtively (for it was taken for granted that the adult world must know nothing of the Event), they collected such of their possessions as they did not wish to be parted from or such household oddments as they thought might not be missed and set off to join the Outlaws in the old barn in readiness for the coming flood.

Arabella Simpkin brought her two-year-old brother, Fred, in his push-chair. Fred, clasping a bucket in one hand and a spade in the other, was almost hidden by Arabella's dressing-gown, from which protruded a coal-shovel and a broken-ribbed umbrella.

Caroline Jones brought a couple of dusters, a dishcloth, a plastic pail, and a teddy bear.

Ella Poppleham brought her fancy dress outfit as Cherry Ripe and a packet of washing-powder.

Georgie Bell trundled a cart on wheels into which he had put his train set and a fingerless clock.

Jimmy Barlow brought his toy boat, a croquet mallet, and a game of ludo.

Bobby Dexter brought his stamp collection, half a dozen comics, and a small bag of potatoes.

Maisie Fellowes carried an outsize 'weaving set' and had a bath towel draped round her shoulders.

Freddie Parker brought a packet of liquorice allsorts and a cucumber.

Launcelot and Geraint, the Thompson twins, brought two dogs, a cat, a hamster and a rabbit.

Frankie Miller followed them, walking slowly and

steadily, carrying a budgerigar in a cage, and behind him straggled various other children, carrying an assortment of personal or household goods.

Arabella headed the procession. William met her at the door, his face set sternly, his brows drawn together in a ferocious scowl.

"You can't come in here," he said.

"Oh, can't I!" said Arabella, shrilly. " 'Oo d'you think you are—Noah or 'Itler or 'oo? We've as much right to it as you 'ave. We've——"

Frankie Miller had pushed his way to the front.

"I thought the budgie would do 'stead of the dove," he said.

"Dove?" said William. "What dove? I don't know what you're talkin' about."

"The dove that came back with the leaf in its mouth in the flood," said Frankie. "He got it off a mountain."

"Flood?" said William. "It's got nothin' to do with a flood."

" 'Course it's to do with a flood," said Arabella. "Don't you try to keep us out of it, William Brown. We know all about it. Mean, that's what you are. Tryin' to keep it all to yourself. Don't care 'oo drowns as long as it isn't you. Dogs in mangers, that's what you are, the lot of you."

"I'll do the washin' up an' the dustin'," said Caroline Jones. "I can clean windows, too."

"We can make fingers for the clock," said Georgie Bell. "I think its inside's all right."

"Yes," shrilled Arabella. "Look at all the stuff we've brought. You ought to be *grateful* 'stead of carryin' on like dogs in mangers."

"You wouldn't know the time without a clock," said Georgie, "an' you ought to know the time in a flood."

"YOU CAN'T COME IN HERE," SAID WILLIAM

"An' you wouldn't know when you'd got to this mountain without the budgie," said Frankie Miller. "You'd go on sailin' an' sailing' for ever an' ever . . . An' it *talks*. It *says* things. It's *comp'ny*. An' it won't be any trouble. I've brought it bird-seed in my pocket."

"An' we're not goin' to be kept out of it, William Brown," said Arabella. "I've been tellin' Fred all about it an' he's brought his bucket an' spade for the seaside. So *there*! Come on!"

"Get *out*!" said William savagely, but Arabella and her followers surged forward and in a few moments the invasion was in full swing.

Arabella and William were carrying on a lively skirmish with coal-shovel and broom-handle. Caroline Jones was trying to fix her plastic pail over Ginger's head, while Ginger was hitting out wildly but ineffectually with his tennis racket. Maisie Fellowes was prodding Douglas in the stomach with her weaving set and Douglas was holding her off as best he could with the toasting-fork. Ella Poppleham, intoxicated by the excitement of battle, was scattering washing-powder over everyone within range, while Jimmy Barlow and Frankie Dakers were fighting for the possession of the motor-tyre. George Bell was drawing long discordant strains from Henry's trumpet and Bobby Dexter was giving a passable imitation of his father's golf stroke with the croquet mallet and the tin of baked beans. Jumble and the Thompson dogs were engaged in what appeared to be a fight-to-the-finish, and the Thompson cat was getting in a few good scratches whenever opportunity allowed. The hamster had taken refuge under Geraint's sweater and the rabbit was quietly eating Douglas's cabbage in a corner. The Thompson twins wore their usual air of detachment. Launcelot was reading Bobby Dexter's comics, and Geraint was playing a game of ludo against himself.

The sounds of shouting, screaming, trumpet-blowing and snarling (increased by indignant yells from Fred, who had suddenly realised that no one was in attendance on him) rose to a *crescendo*.

"Get *out*!" shouted William, parrying a blow from Arabella's coal-shovel. "Get *out* all of you!"

Then suddenly he saw that a couple of men were setting up a camera just outside the doorway, and that another man was standing in the doorway watching the scene with a slightly puzzled air. William freed himself from Arabella and approached the newcomer.

"What d'you want?" he said fiercely. "It's private here."

"Who's in charge of all this?" said the man.

"Me," said William.

"It's—it's a Children's Holiday Play Centre, I take it," said the man.

"Yes," said William, deciding that it might as well be that as anything else.

"And you're in charge of it?"

"Yes," said William, feeling no doubts at all on that score.

"Well, you see," said the man, "we're doing a documentary on Children's Holiday Play Centres."

"D'you mean for the telly?" said William.

"Yes. We've done a selection that we'd arranged beforehand, but they were all run and organised by adults and we rather wanted to find one that's run and organised by the children themselves. We've got a roving commission and plenty of time so, when we were driving along the road and saw all these children making their way here and carrying various articles, we thought it was worth investigating. So it's a Play Centre and you're the organiser?"

"Yes," said William. "It's a Play Centre an' I'm the organiser."

His voice was deeply magisterial, his expression earnest and authoritative. He was no longer a survivor of an atomic war. He was an organiser of a Children's Holiday Play Centre.

"Oh, well . . ." said the man. He still looked puzzled and a little doubtful. "We might as well get on with it. Now I'd like to ask you a few questions first. Answer them into the mike." He drew William a little way out of the barn, held the microphone to his lips and raised his voice so as to be heard above the uproar.

"So you're the boy who has organised this Holiday Play Centre for the children of the neighbourhood?"

"Yes," said William simply. "I'm him."

The man's eyes roved over the crowd of screaming scuffling children.

"They all seem to be doing different things," he said.

"Yes, I've set 'em on doin' diff'rent things," said William.

"Two of them seem to be having a wrestling match."

"Yes, I've set 'em on havin' a wrestling match," said William.

"Rather noisy, aren't they?"

"Yes, I've set 'em on bein' noisy," said William. "It's good for 'em."

"Free expression, I suppose!" said the man.

"Oh yes, it's all free," said William.

"One of them seems to be putting a bucket over another's head," said the man. "Is that a game?"

"Yes," said William. "It's a new game I've invented for them."

"Some of them seem to be throwing potatoes at each other."

"Yes," said William. "That's another new game I've invented for them."

"One of them seems to be lassooing another with a motor-tyre."

"Yes," said William. "That's another new game I've invented for them. I've invented a lot of new games for them."

"And the one with the roller skates . . . Ah, here's one of them coming to look for you."

Arabella, still armed with the coal-shovel, was emerging from the crowd, her face alight with the lust of battle, her eyes fixed ominously on William.

"Now, little girl," said the man. "I'd like to ask you a few questions about this Play Centre. This little boy's explained that he's the organiser of the whole scheme and I think it does great credit to you all." He winced as a blast from the trumpet blended with a yell from Fred. "Now please answer into the microphone." He held the microphone to her lips. "Are you enjoying this Play Centre, organised by this little boy?"

"*What?*" shrilled Arabella.

Nervously the man repeated the question.

"*What?*" said Arabella again. "I'm organising anythin' but devilment an' monkeyin' about? 'Oo does 'e think 'e is? Oh yes, we can all drown, can't we, for all 'e cares. 'E's the only one that matters, gettin' away from it all in 'is ark. An' where *is* 'is ark, that's what I want to know. Got all the stuff for it, but where *is* it?" She fixed her furious gaze on the man. "Where *is* it? Jus' tell me that."

The man had withdrawn the microphone. His nervousness was increasing. He was looking round as if for escape when suddenly Fred appeared. His push-chair had been overturned and he had extricated himself from it with difficulty. His yells rose deafeningly above the tumult.

"What's the matter, little boy?" said the man.

"Hungry," bawled Fred. "*Hungry!*"

"He says he's hungry," explained Arabella.

Arabella had accustomed herself to translate Fred's imperfect speech throughout his infancy, and, though now he could articulate more or less distinctly, she could not break herself of the habit.

Fred gathered breath for another deafening howl. Hastily the man took a bar of chocolate from his pocket and handed it to him.

"There you are, my little man," he said.

But a fresh force of invaders was surging across the field. It was led by Arabella's mother, and the mothers of the other children followed. They had been attending a meeting of the Women's League, at which a talk had been given on "Life in Instanbul" by a friend of a friend of the Vicar's, who had once spent a night there, and they had returned to find their children vanished, together with various odds and ends of household equipment. A few inquiries had led them to the scene of the drama. Arabella's mother stalked up to the man with the microphone, her lips grimly set.

"An' what d'you think *you're* doin'?" she said, "lurin' our kids away to make a telly commercial of them without so much as by your leave. Well, we've caught you at it, 'aven't we, good an' proper, an' you'll 'ave to pay up or we'll 'ave the lor on you." Threatening murmurs of assent came from the other women. "You can't deny it. We seed you with our own eyes givin' that bar of chocolate to our Fred, in front of them cameras an' all. I don't know *'oo's* make of chocolate you're advertisin' an' I don't care. All I knows is them kids on commercials gets paid top money an' I'll see our Fred gets it, too."

"My good woman," said the man desperately, "Let me explain——"

**ARABELLA'S MOTHER STALKED UP TO THE MAN WITH THE
MICROPHONE.**

"Oh, yes, you'll 'ave a fine story to tell, I've no doubt,"
said Arabella's mother with a high-pitched sarcastic laugh,
"but we caught you in the act all right, didn't we?" Again
her followers gave a murmur of assent. They were finding
it more interesting than "Life in Istanbul".

"Ought to be ashamed of yourselves, you did! Usin'
the poor kids! Imposin' on their ignorance! Grindin' the
faces of the poor! Tryin' to do commercials on the sly to
get out of payin' for 'em, but the lor's the lor an' you'll
find that out before we've finished with you."

"But, my good woman, do please, listen . . ." said the
man frantically.

The pandemonium in the barn had died away. The

children were crowding into the doorway to watch the scene.

All except four.

William, Ginger, Henry and Douglas, followed by Jumble (who had torn himself away from his dog-fight to accompany them) had scraped through the hedge and were making their way as unobtrusively as possible across the next field down to the road. Nearing the road, they stopped to listen. The sound of the upraised voice of Arabella's mother and the barking of the Thompson dogs filled the air.

"Gosh!" said William.

"Thank goodness our mothers weren't there!" said Ginger.

"Mine was finishin' off her Spring cleanin'," said William.

"Mine was plantin' out her petunias," said Douglas.

"Mine said that life in this village was enough for her without botherin' about Istanbul," said Henry.

"But they'll get to know," said William.

"An' they'll blame us for it," said Ginger.

"An' it was nothin' to do with us," said William. "We didn't *ask* them to come. We were jus' having' a nice quiet game by ourselves when they came bargin' in an' messin' everythin' up."

They walked on for a few yards then stopped again to listen. The tumult was dying down again, replaced by a babble of children's voices. Above the babble the words "William Brown" could be clearly distinguished.

"There!" said William. There was a certain gloomy satisfaction in his voice. "I *knew* they'd say it was my fault. Nothin' ever happens anywhere without them sayin' it was my fault."

"It wasn't any of our faults," said Ginger.

"Course it wasn't," said William. "We did nothin'."

"Nothin'," said Ginger.

"Nothin'," said Henry.

"Nothin'," said Douglas.

"Well, let's try'n' *look* as if we'd done nothin'," said William. "That sometimes helps. To start with anyway."

He brushed down his jacket, removing the traces of Arabella's coal-shovel as best he could, smoothed back his hair and composed his features. The others followed his example. Even Jumble, realising that danger and disgrace were threatening, hastened to put on the Faithful Hound look that had got him out of many a tight corner.

Then, slowly and decorously, their eyes fixed dreamily on the far horizon, their faces alight with innocence, they proceeded on their homeward way . . .

Chapter 2

William and the Disappearing Manuscripts

General Moult's ninetieth birthday was approaching and everyone in the village was aware of it except General Moult. General Moult had lost interest in his age. He'd forgotten the exact date of his birthday and couldn't be bothered to keep pace with the passing years. He'd managed it till he was eighty and then he'd given up the attempt. He'd stopped at eighty. It was a good round number and he'd got used to it. He disliked change of any sort.

It was Miss Roundway who, prowling about various Record Offices on private genealogical investigations of her own, had suddenly taken it into her head to investigate the matter of the General's age and had discovered that he would be ninety years old the next week. The news spread quickly through the village, but any approach to the General himself was met by a testy, "Rubbish! Nonsense! Won't hear a word of it!"

It happened that everyone was feeling a little flat. The

spate of summer festivities was over and the spate of Christmas festivities had not yet begun, so the idea of a Birthday Celebration fired the imagination of the village . . . and when anything fired the imagination of the village it took more than a little testiness to damp it down.

A committee—Mrs. Monks, Mrs. Bott, Miss Milton, Miss Roundway and Miss Thompson—appointed itself and met in the Vicarage drawing-room to discuss the details.

Mrs. Monks opened proceedings by reading a passage from a book called *The Magic of Africa* that had been among the left-overs from her last Jumble Sale.

" 'Nature has poured out her riches unstintingly upon this exquisite corner of the earth, this gem of tropical beauty. Her noble hills, her lush valleys, her majestic uplands, her winding rivers, the beauty of sunrise and sunset, the wonder of flora and fauna . . .' " She turned over a page uncertainly. "Well, it just goes on like that."

"Doesn't seem much point in it," said Miss Milton.

"And there's other things in Africa than them," said Mrs. Bott darkly.

"I know, I know," said Mrs. Monks, "but, you see, the General fought in the South African War and the South African War is the subject of the memoirs he's writing now, so I felt we must keep the thought of South Africa in our minds—to set the atmosphere, as it were—while we discuss the celebration."

"What sort of celebration do you think of having?" said Miss Roundway.

"That's what we're here to discuss," said Mrs. Monks.

"A party of some sort, I suppose," said Miss Milton.

"He won't come to it," said Miss Roundway. "He nearly snapped my head off when I just mentioned it."

"It seems silly to have a party for him if he's not going to come to it," said Miss Thompson.

"He doesn't know he's ninety, you see," said Miss Roundway. "He thinks he's eighty."

"We could *prove* it," said Miss Thompson.

"That wouldn't help," said Miss Roundway.

"But we *must* have some sort of celebration for him," said Mrs. Monks. "There can't be many of these South African War veterans left. He's given his *life* to South Africa, in a manner of speaking. First the war and then his memoirs. He's been writing his memoirs for *years*. He's a National Figure. And he's a Literary Figure, too. We must do him honour as a famous member of our little community."

"There's fireworks," said Miss Thompson. "They're pretty. We could get up a firework display in his garden."

"He probably wouldn't notice it," said Miss Milton.

"And it would rain anyway," said Mrs. Monks.

"I could show those coloured photographs I took in the Isle of Wight," said Mrs. Bott. "Botty gave me a projector and I haven't tried it out yet. They might remind him of South Africa. After all, scenery's scenery all the world over."

"No, no, no!" said Mrs. Monks.

"Oh, all right!" said Mrs. Bott huffily.

"Some people from Canada whom I met the other week," said Miss Roundway, "were telling me of a very charming custom they have there for birthday celebrations and things like that. They take the whole feast over to the person's house as a sort of surprise and have the party in the person's house. It means no trouble or expense to the person and it's such a lovely surprise."

They considered the suggestion in silence for a few moments.

"Suppose the person's out," said Mrs. Monks at last.

"I expect they make some sort of provision for that," said Miss Roundway vaguely.

"He wouldn't let us in even if he was there," said Miss Milton, "and we'd look rather silly just carrying the feast away and eating it by ourselves somewhere else."

"There's a picture of the Needles that might have been done by an artist," said Mrs Bott.

"His house is too small for a party, anyway," said Miss Milton.

"We might have it in the Village Hall," said Mrs. Monks.

"What would be the point of that?" said Mrs. Milton. "He wouldn't come."

"We might *lure* him," said Miss Roundway. "Get him there on some pretext and then persuade him to stay."

"What pretext?" said Mrs. Monks.

Again they considered the question in silence.

"There's the window-catch," suggested Miss Thompson.

On the last of the many occasions on which the General had given his well-known "talk" on South Africa, he had been irritated by the rattling of a window just behind him on the platform. The next morning he had fixed a new patent catch, which had a habit of refusing to function every now and then for no apparent reason. Only the General seemed able to deal with it.

"We could pretend it had gone wrong again," said Miss Thompson.

"And it probably would have done," said Miss Milton.

"Well, the birthday's next Wednesday," said Mrs. Monks, "so we must hurry on with our arrangements. We——"

She was interrupted by a loud and raucous shout from

the garden. They turned to see a boy crossing the lawn
in a series of running leaps that failed to clear the bed of
calceolarias, landed him into the middle of a small colony
of mixed asters and finally dispatched him through a hole
in the hedge, still shouting lustily as he vanished from
view.

"Who on earth was that?" said Miss Roundway.

"William Brown," said Mrs. Monks bitterly. "Who else
could it have been?"

William arrived first at the cross-roads. Ginger joined him
a few moments later. They stood for a moment or two to
recover their breath.

"I won," panted William at last.

"You cheated," said Ginger. "You cut through the
Vicarage garden."

"Well, I yelled out to you I was goin' to," ' said
William. "You could have done it too."

"You'll get into a row," said Ginger. "Did anyone see
you?"

"Yes, there was a whole crowd of them in there," said
William. "I don't know what they were doin'."

"I know," said Ginger. "My mother was talkin' about
it. It's about Gen'ral Moult."

"What about him?" said William.

"They're goin' to have a birthday party for him nex'
week when he's ninety an' he won't go to it."

"Why not?"

" 'Cause he doesn't know he's ninety for one thing an'
he doesn't like parties for another."

"They're all right sometimes," said William. "It
depends . . ."

"Yes," agreed Ginger. "Some of them have good food
an' rotten games an' some have rotten food an' good

games. You don't often get 'em both together, but I did once. I once went to a party where they had five diff'rent colours of jelly an' played Lions an' Tamers."

"That was jolly good," said William, "but about Gen'ral Moult . . ."

"I met him yesterday," said Ginger, "an' he jus' glared at me."

"He always does," said William.

"Yes, but it was a *special* sort of glare," said Ginger. "He wasn't glarin' *at* me, he was jus' glarin'—as if he was sort of scared."

"Scared?" said William. "Him? . . . I say! We've not got anythin' partic'lar to do this morning have we? Let's go to his house an' see if anythin's happenin'. I bet Mr. Mason'll be somewhere around."

Mason had served under the General in the South African War. He was his secretary cum companion cum valet cum gardener and a great friend of the Outlaws. His real name was Aaron Mason, but the General considered the name Aaron "unsuitable" and had renamed him Bill.

They found him in the garden hoeing the rose bed. He was a small, slight man with yellow wizened face and twinkling blue eyes.

" 'Ello, 'ello, 'ello!" he said when he saw them at the gate. "An 'ow are you?"

"All right, thanks," said William.

"And how are you, Mr. Mason?" said Ginger, who sometimes remembered his manners.

"Worried," said Bill, his features clouding over.

"What are you worried about?" said William.

"The Gen'ral," said Bill, lowering his voice and glancing round. "Come on in an' I'll tell you."

They opened the little green-and-white gate and entered the garden.

"I don't think 'e's back from 'is walk yet," said Bill, resting on his hoe. "You'll 'ave to run off if 'e comes so I'll tell you quick . . . It's 'is memoirs."

"D'you mean the ones he's been writin' for years?" said William.

"Yes," said Bill. "Forty or fifty notebooks of diaries, 'e'd got. No end to them, there wasn't. They'd have 'alf filled the Albert 'All . . . Well, las' year 'e got the idea of 'avin' them published. 'E kept it a secret, 'cept from me, 'cause—well, I s'pose 'e wanted to spring it on people after it was all fixed up."

"I'd feel like that, too," said William.

"Yes, so would I," agreed Ginger. "They'd—they'd have to take you a bit more *seriously* after that."

"Well, you know 'e thinks the South African War was the finest war in history," said Bill, "an I feel that way about it myself too. We was fightin' man against man in God's open country without tanks or atom bombs or any such like contraptions. Them other two wars wasn't a patch on it. An' the Gen'ral wanted to—sort of pay 'is respects to it, let people know 'ow 'e felt about it an' get them to feel the same. 'E 'ad to cut it down a bit to start with, of course."

"That'd take a bit of doin'," said William.

"Yes, it did. Day after day, night after night, 'e was at it, cuttin' it down, messin' about with it this way an' that to get it short enough to fit into a book. Nearly broke 'is 'eart, it did, but 'e kept on at it. 'E did it. 'Is duty to posterity, 'e said it was. Same as a precious 'eritage 'e'd got to 'and down to 'em, keepin' it alive in their memory so's it'd never be forgot."

"When is it goin' to be printed?" said William.

Bill shook his head sadly.

"That's the trouble," he said. "It keeps comin' back. 'E sends it out to publisher after publisher an' it always comes back. It's as if there was some sort of hoo-doo on it an'—an' 'e's beginning' to think there *is* one."

"What's a hoo-doo?" said Ginger.

"A sort of evil spell put on somethin' by a witch doctor."

"Do you mean a *partic'lar* witch doctor?" said William.

"Yes," said Bill. "'E thinks it's this witch doctor what 'e knew in South Africa. Once 'e 'ad 'im arrested for somethin' an' put 'im in jail an' 'e was out nex' mornin' though there wasn't any way 'e *could* 'ave got out. No one could ever keep 'im in any sort of prison an' bad luck followed anyone that annoyed him."

"Well, the Gen'ral couldn't have annoyed him all this time afterwards," said Ginger.

"Yes, 'e could an' 'e thinks 'e 'as done," said Bill mournfully. "You see, 'e's put a whole chapter about 'im an' the wicked things 'e did—murder an' such like. You see, 'e thought it was part of this duty to posterity to tell the truth, the whole truth, an' nothin' but the truth. 'E took this witch doctor chapter out of the book once 'cause 'e thought this witch doctor was on 'is track to pay 'im out for givin' away 'is secrets, but 'is conscience made 'im put it in again."

"But the witch doctor couldn't get at him here—all this way off,' said William.

Bill shook his head.

"Time an' place means nothin' to them," he said. "They can get themselves 'ere, there an' everywhere, whenever they've a mind to. An' the Gen'ral's gettin' surer an' surer it's this witch doctor that's gettin' 'is book sent back from wherever 'e sends it to. An' "—Bill sank his voice mysteriously—"you'll 'ardly believe this but 'e's beginnin' to think that this witch doctor's come over 'ere after 'im."

"D'you mean *here*?" said William.

"To this *village*?" said Ginger.

"Yes, 'ere," said Bill. "To this village. An' 'e thinks 'e's seen 'im!"

"Seen the witch doctor?" gasped William.

"Yes. 'E thinks 'e's the man what's taken that cottage that's almost 'idden by the trees. Martyn Cottage, it's called. 'E's got deep black eyes an' 'e's thin an' narrer same as this witch doctor was an' the Gen'ral thinks 'e *is* the witch doctor come over 'ere to stop 'im gettin' this book published."

"But how *could* he?" said William.

Bill shook his head.

"They've got ways you'd never believe," he said. "Spells an' things . . . The Gen'ral's started 'idin' this manuscript so's this witch doctor won't get at it an' then 'e forgets where 'e's 'id it. 'E 'id it in the dustbin the other day 'cause 'e thought the witch doctor'd never track it down there an' then 'e forgot 'e'd put it there an' I only jus' stopped the dustman makin' off with it. 'E gets worse tempered every day. 'E doesn't eat or sleep for worryin' an' 'e's gettin' me as bad as what 'e is 'isself . . .'Ere 'e is! You'd better clear off."

General Moult came in at the garden gate. His face seemed to have grown thinner than it had been the last time the boys had seen him. His mouth was grimly set, his eyes pouched and red-rimmed. His drooping moustache drooped more dejectedly than ever. His eyes blazed with anger when he saw the two boys.

"Get out!" he said, raising his stick threateningly. "Get out, both of you! How dare you come trespassing on my property! How *dare* you! Get *out*!"

He entered the front door abruptly. Bill followed, turning to make a gesture of helplessness before he closed the door.

"GET OUT!" HE SAID, RAISING HIS STICK THREATENINGLY.

William and Ginger walked slowly down the road.

"Well, it's jolly serious," said William.

"But it can't be true," said Ginger. "I mean, there can't really be people like witch doctors. We thought we'd found a witch once—d'you remember?—an' she turned out not to be one."

"Yes, but that was diff'rent," said William. "There *aren't* witches really, 'cept in fairy tales, but witch doctors are diff'rent. There *are* them. The Gen'ral's met them an' spoken to them. He *knows* them an' their goin's-on. They can do awful things like killin' people at a distance."

"Gosh!" said Ginger. "Well, I think we'd better not get mixed up in it. There's nothin' we can do, anyway."

"I s'pose not," said William a little regretfully, "but we'll keep a look-out."

He kicked a stone from one side of the road to the other, picked it up, took aim at a conker that dangled temptingly over the road, missed it, tried to do a handspring on the grass verge, overbalanced and stood up to see Victor Jameson coming round the bend of the road.

"Hello," said Victor.

"Hello," said William.

"What've you been doin'?" said Victor, who was always interested in William's activities.

"Nothin'," said William. "What've you been doin'?"

"Givin' out notices," said Victor.

"What sort of notices?" said William.

"Notices of the next Jumble Sale," said Victor. "My mother's given me a shilling for taking them round to every house in the village an' I'm just about worn out. I should think I've walked more than a hundred miles." A thoughtful look came into his face. "I say . . ."

"Yes?"

"That's a funny chap living down at Martyn Cottage."

"How d'you mean, funny?" said William.

"Well, I had to pass the sitting-room window to get to the front door and there he was dancin'!"

"Dancin'!" said William.

"Yes. Dancin' about the room all by himself. He's probably escaped from some asylum. Dancin' about the room. All by himself . . . He'd got a foreign sort of look, too . . . Oh well, I'll be goin' on home an' get something to eat. I'm nearly dead of starvation with all this walkin' about on an empty stomach. Well, nearly empty, anyway."

He went on down the road. William and Ginger stood and looked at each other.

"Well," said William. "That *proves* it, doesn't it?"

"Proves what?"

"Proves he's the witch doctor. I saw a picture of them once on the telly doin' devil dances to work their spells. It *proves* he's that witch doctor an' that he's after the Gen'ral's manuscript. He was doin' this devil dance to *get* it. P'raps this dance'd sort of *hypnotise* the Gen'ral an' make him *take* it to him."

"I bet it'd take more than a devil dance to hypnotise the Gen'ral," said Ginger.

"Well, we'll go on keepin' a look-out," said William.

They continued to keep a look-out, but it was not till the following Tuesday—the day before the General's birthday—that their suspicions seemed to be justified.

Making their way to the General's house in the course of the afternoon, they met a slender figure with deep-set eyes walking swiftly and purposefully along the road. He threw them a quick piercing glance as he passed them. They stopped to gaze after him.

"It's him all right," said William.

"Yes, it mus' be," agreed Ginger.

"An' he's been to the Gen'ral's house," said William.

"We don't *know* he has," said Ginger.

"Well, he came from that direction, so he *mus'* have been. He couldn't have come from anywhere else."

"He might have done," said Ginger.

"Well, I bet he didn't," said William. "You could tell by the look on his face that he'd been up to some devilry . . . Let's go'n' have a look."

They went down the lane and opened the little green-and-white gate that led into the General's garden. There was no one about.

"Mr. Mason!" called William on a low urgent note.

An upstairs window was thrown open and Bill's head appeared. His face wore a woebegone expression.

"We've seen him," said William, "comin' away from this d'rection. Has he been here?"

"Don't think so," said Bill. "I've got me lumbago somethin' cruel. Doctor says I've got to rest today. Can't 'ardly move, anyway."

"Gosh, that's bad luck!" said William. "How's the Gen'ral?"

" 'E's in an awful way this mornin'. Didn't sleep. Didn't 'ave no breakfast. Went off mutterin' to isself. 'E'll be stark ravin' mad in a day or two. So'll I . . . Now off you go, kids. I'll try'n' drag meself round to make 'is bed."

He withdrew his head and closed the window.

"We've *got* to do somethin' now," said William in a tone of finality. "The Gen'ral's goin' mad an' Mr. Mason's got lumbago, so we're the only ones left to do it."

"What can we do?" said Ginger.

"First of all we've got to find out if this witch doctor's been here this mornin'."

"Mr. Mason said he didn't think he had," said Ginger.

"LOOK!" HE SAID. "THAT WASN'T THERE YESTERDAY."

"He didn't *know*," said William. "We've got to make sure. We'll have a good look round. He might have left some clue. We'll look in the greenhouse first."

They went to the open greenhouse door.

William gasped.

"Look!" he said, pointing to a cardboard box beneath the stage just opposite. "That wasn't there yesterday."

"How d'you know it wasn't?"

"I took a look round when I was passing an' I noticed particular that that place was empty. I remember thinkin' it'd make a good clear run for a train set. Let's look at it."

They approached the box somewhat warily. It was a cardboard box fastened by wire. On it was written "A PRESENT FROM SOUTH AFRICA."

"It's him," said William. "He's *been*! I knew he had. I could tell by his face that he'd been. He's put it there. There's prob'ly some sort of spell on it—might even be a bomb that'd go off the minute the Gen'ral opened it. That 'PRESENT FROM SOUTH AFRICA' is a sort of sign that it comes from the witch doctor. It's a sort of *threat*."

"We could put it in Jenks's pond," said Ginger.

"No," said William. "We've got to do somethin' to scare him, to show we're on his track . . . Let's take it back to his house."

"Gosh, William, we *can't*."

"Yes, we can. We know where he's stayin'. We'll take it there. It might turn the curse back on him 'stead of on the Gen'ral. Anyway, he'll know we've sort of declared war on him . . . Come on!"

They made their way slowly and cautiously to Martyn Cottage—William adopting an odd, crablike gait as he tried to clasp the box firmly to him and at the same time keep a safe distance from it.

"It's jolly dangerous, you know," said Ginger.

"I've done dangerouser things than this," said William. "I once tracked down an international spy."

"He turned out not to be one," Ginger reminded him.

"Well, that wasn't my fault," said William. "Anyway, I bet this witch doctor stuff'll be all right."

They had reached Martyn Cottage. Gate and front door stood invitingly open.

"Come on!" said William.

"You'd better knock," said Ginger.

William approached the front door and performed his resounding tattoo on the knocker. The echoes died away into silence.

"There's no one in," he said. "Come on!"

He entered the hall, followed by Ginger, and pushed open the first door on the right. It was a small room, sparsely furnished by a desk, armchair and table. He placed the box in the middle of the hearth rug.

"He'll see it as soon as he comes in," he said, "an' he'll know that we've declared war on him. I bet he'll be scared. I bet he'll be so scared he'll go back to wherever he came from. He'll think we've got more witch doctor stuff than he has." He wandered around the room, inspecting its contents. "I wonder what's in here." He took up a cardboard box from the desk and opened it. It was full of loose sheets of manuscript. He turned them over. They were covered with strange and apparently meaningless hieroglyphics, scrawled at random, as it seemed, across each page.

"Gosh!" said William in a faint, awestruck voice. "It's his book of spells. It mus' be his book of spells. It couldn't be anythin' else. Let's take it. He'll be helpless without his book of spells. Come on quick before he gets back."

He replaced the pages of manuscript in the box, took it up and went to the door. Ginger followed, glancing round apprehensively.

"We can't bother about danger," said William. "It's war. You don't bother about danger in war. Think of Nelson an' that man that charged the Light Brigade an' that man called Horatius that kept that bridge back in the Stone Age."

"It wasn't in the Stone Age," said Ginger. "It was in the brave days of old."

"Comes to the same thing," said William. "Anyway, let's get away before he finds out."

They walked quickly down the road. Suddenly William stopped.

"Gosh!" he said.

The tenant of Martyn Cottage was approaching them . . . Again he threw them a quick glance from dark deep-set eyes as he passed.

"Good thing he didn't notice the box," said Ginger.

"He'll soon find out about it," said William, who always liked to savour danger to the full. "He'll go home an' find it gone an' then he'll remember meetin' us with it. We're practically in the jaws of death already."

"But he won't be able to do anythin' without his spell book," said Ginger.

"Not at first," said William, "but he won't give in without a struggle. He'll bide his time an' gather his powers together, but as long as we've got the book——"

"What are we goin' to do with it?" said Ginger.

William stopped for a moment or two to consider.

"We ought to destroy it," he said. "Hidin' it's no use. We've got to destroy its power. Burnin' would be best . . ."

"How can we burn it?" said Ginger. "Someone'd be sure to see an' start makin' a fuss."

"A garden fire'd be the best place," said William. "No one would know it wasn't an ordin'ry bonfire. Its evil would go right up into the air with the smoke an' be lost for ever . . . I *say*!"

"Yes?"

"There's a rubbish heap at the bottom of the Gen'ral's garden. Let's put it on that, then when they light it, it'll get burnt up with all the other rubbish an' that'll be the end of it. We won't tell Mr. Mason till it's over. He's all right but he's a grown-up an' grown-ups can't stop interferin'. It's their nature. They can't help it. Besides, he's got lumbago an' the Gen'ral's goin' mad, so it only leaves us. Let's go'n' see if there's anyone about."

They had reached the General's house and stood in

the gateway looking cautiously around. The garden was empty. No one could be seen at the windows.

"Let's do it quick," whispered William. "*Quick* before anyone comes."

They crept round the side of the house to the back garden. There—on a piece of rough ground at the end of the lawn—stood the rubbish heap, crowned by a pile of freshly gathered dead leaves.

"We won't dig it in deep," said William. "It'd take too long an' someone might come an' catch us at it. Let's jus' stick it under the leaves on the top. They'll cover it up an' it'll burn with them an' that'll be the end of *him* an' his witch doctorin'."

It was the work of a few moments to go down to the heap and thrust the cardboard box beneath the leaves. Quickly they returned to the front gate, then—just as they were opening it—Bill emerged from the front door.

" 'Ello, 'ello, 'ello," he said. "Anythin' I can do for you?"

"No, thank you," said William. "We've jus' come to—we've jus' come to—well," with a sudden burst of inspiration—"to see how you are."

"I'm fine, thanks," said Bill. "Me lumbago's all but wore off, but the General's in a bad way."

"Why?"

" 'E's 'id 'is manuscript somewhere again an' he's forgot where 'e 'id it. We've turned the whole place upside-down lookin' for it an' we can't find it nowhere. 'E keeps on about this witch doctor. Says 'e'll be 'aunted by bad luck till 'e's took the chapter out an' 'e's not goin' to do it. Keeps sayin' 'e's got this duty to posterity an' 'e's goin' through with it. It's my opinion 'e'll end up in a luny bin an' me with 'im."

"Well, he needn't worry," said William mysteriously,

"tell him he needn't worry. Tell him we've got it all fixed up an'—an' he needn't worry."

Bill grinned.

"Right!" he said. "I'll tell 'im all 'is troubles is at an end."

"Yes, and they really *are*," said William.

"He'll soon *know* they are," said Ginger.

"Oh and—er—by the way," said William with an elaborate pretence of unconcern. "We've jus'—well, we jus' wondered when you were goin' to have a bonfire."

"Tomorrow afternoon, if I can get down to it," said Bill. "Why? You comin' along to give a hand?"

"We've not much to do tomorrow," said William with a still more elaborate air of unconcern, "so we jus' poss'bly might."

They set out for the General's house the next afternoon . . . slowing their pace as they approached it.

"I can see the rubbish heap," said Ginger. "He's not started the bonfire."

"Good!" said William. "We can keep him talking while he's doin' it so that——" He seized Ginger suddenly by his arm and dragged him into the cover of the hedge. "Look!" he whispered. "Look! It's him!"

Ginger looked. The tenant of Martyn Cottage was walking nimbly and briskly along the road. He stopped at the green-and-white gate, hesitated for a moment or two, then opened it, walked up the little path and knocked at the front door.

"He's come for his spell book," whispered William, "an 'e'll stick at nothin' to get it."

"What can we do?" said Ginger.

"We'll go round to the back," said William. "We can hide between the window an' that bush that grows there an' keep an eye on things. No one'll see us there an' we can rescue the Gen'ral if deadly peril closes in on him."

They made their way to the back of the house and crouched behind the bush. With a little manoeuvring they could see into the room where the General and his visitor stood confronting each other. The General's face was flushed, his eyes blazed, his drooping moustache seemed to bristle with rage.

"I don't know what you're talking about," he was saying. "If you try any of your devil's tricks on me . . ."

"I'm trying to explain," said the young man patiently. "I'm a dancer and a choreographer—of some repute I may add. At present I'm arranging some ballet dances for a forthcoming production and I've come down here in order to work in peace away from the distractions of town life, but my notes, which are invaluable to me in the preparation of the ballet, have disappeared. I use a private sort of shorthand of my own invention to describe the steps. It could mean nothing to anyone else, and I am helpless without it. It contains the work of months. I kept the loose sheets in a cardboard box and it has disappeared."

"And what has this to do with me?" spluttered the General. "How dare you come here insinuating . . ."

"I'm insinuating nothing," said the young man. "I only say that I passed two boys in the road yesterday carrying a cardboard box and it wasn't till I looked for my own box last night and couldn't find it that I realised that the box the boys were carrying was mine. I made inquiries and found that the boys had been seen by a passer-by entering your gate with the box."

A movement at the bottom of the garden attracted his attention and he turned sharply to look out of the window. A man stood by the rubbish heap with a rake in his hand.

He was evidently going to arrange the contents of the heap in a manner more convenient for burning. He raised the rake and began to draw down the heaped leaves from the top.

The young man leapt to his feet with a loud cry, sprang through the open window, flew as if on wings down the garden and snatched up a cardboard box that was sliding down the heap. He returned to the room clasping it to his breast, flung it on to the hearthrug, fell on his knees beside it and tore off the lid, revealing pages covered with lines and dots and squiggles . . . He gave a long-drawn sigh of relief.

"My precious notes! My dances!" he cried. "But what happened?" He pointed an accusing finger at the General. "Why did you do it? *Why* did you steal it? *Why* did you try to burn it? *Why* did you plot and plan to ruin my career?"

The General was almost past the power of speech. He could only stammer, "I-I-I didn't . . ."

The young man continued with unabated eloquence:

"What about those two boys you suborned to perform the theft? They would confute you if only I could lay my hands on them. They——"

Again a faint sound from outside attracted his attention. Again he turned to the window . . . William and Ginger had forgotten caution in their excitement. Their heads were plainly visible above the top of the laurel bush. The dancer, who was surprisingly strong despite his slender build, seized them and dragged them into the room.

'Now deny it if you can," he said to the General. "Deny that you hired these boys to steal my choreographic notes, to bring them to your house, to——"

'Silence!" bellowed the General. The power of speech

had returned to him. He had drawn himself up to his full height. Outraged dignity showed in every line of his figure. His fear and bewilderment had vanished. Here was no witch doctor. Here was simply an impudent young man who needed putting in his place.

"How *dare* you insult me in this way! I am one of Her Majesty's Officers. My name and details of my service can be verified in the records of the War Office. General Moult of . . ."

But the young man was gazing at him, open-eyed, open-mouthed.

"Not General Moult!" he gasped. "Not General *Moult*!"

"Why not, Sir?" said the General, his whole person still rigid with anger.

"You—you wrote those memoirs?" said the young man.

The General gulped and swallowed.

"I have written my memoirs, certainly," he said with dignity. "but I regret to say that I have mislaid them, I . . ."

"No, no," said the young man. "I have them. They are in my house in a box with 'A PRESENT FROM SOUTH AFRICA' on the outside."

The General was silent for a moment or two, then he raised his hand to his head.

"I remember," he said. "I remember now . . . I hid them there. I befriended a child in South Africa during the Boer War and he continues to send me presents each year, always in a box with 'A PRESENT FROM SOUTH AFRICA' on the outside. I remember now. It was just the same size as my manuscript so I hid it there and sealed it firmly. I hid it because . . ."

"But listen," the young man was saying excitedly.

"Listen! Have you made any arrangements for its publication?"

"No," said the General. "Up to the present moment, no."

"Well, listen," said the young man again. "A friend of mine who's a publisher was staying the night with me and he read your manuscript and wants to publish it. The name General Moult was on the manuscript but there was no address, so we didn't know how to get in touch with you . . . This publisher wants to publish a series of war memoirs written during each war—or as many as he can get hold of. He's got one on the Crimean War and others on the two World Wars, but he hasn't yet got one on the South African War. His ultimate aim is to show the essential qualities in the English soldier that survive unchanged by changing surroundings from war to war. He doesn't want anything to do with the strategy or conduct of the war. He just wants the intimate record of one particular type of soldier—simple, upright, conscientious, courageous, with the singleness of purpose, the simplicity of outlook, the dignity, the self-command, the kindliness, that go to make the 'Happy Warrior', you know."

The General was frowning slightly.

"I don't think I'm like that at all," he said.

"They never do," said the young man and continued: "This soldier knows and cares little for the larger aspects of the war, its purpose, its causes, its implications. He simply records the day-by-day events and his reactions to them. Strictly contemporary. No hindsight or know-how. No attempt at any critical assessment of the events, just the events and the soldier's on-the-spot reactions to them. Your memoirs are exactly what this friend of mine wants. Would you be willing to negotiate with him?"

"Thank you," said the General simply. 'I'd be very glad to."

THEY ENTERED THE VILLAGE HALL.

"But these boys . . ." said the young man. "How do they come into it?"

The boys tried to explain but the General cut them short. He felt as if he had awakened from a nightmare. He found it difficult to believe that he had ever given way to such senseless fears.

"Yes, yes, yes," he said, waving the explanations aside impatiently.

"We wanted to help the Gen'ral," said William.

"Well, you seem to've done it all right," said Bill, who had now joined them in order to see what it was all about.

There came a knock at the door. Bill went to answer

"THIS IS YOUR BIRTHDAY PARTY, GENERAL," SAID MISS
MILTON.

it. Miss Milton entered. She wore her best dress and her
lips were set in an ingratiating smile.

"Oh, General," she said, "*would* you kindly come
across to the Village Hall for a moment? The window
catch has gone wrong again."

"Tut tut!" said the General, assuming his usual abrupt
manner. "Will you *never* get the knack of it! All right,
all right, I'll come."

He went down the road to the Village Hall,
accompanied by Miss Milton, the young man, William,
Ginger and Bill.

They entered the Village Hall. It was full of people.

There were tables laden with food and bottles of champagne . . . balloons . . . Union Jacks . . . On a small table in the middle was an iced birthday cake, made by Miss Thompson. She had intended it originally to represent the Victoria Falls but it had gone flat in the making and now represented the Table Mountain.

"This is your birthday party, General," said Miss Milton. "You're ninety years old today."

"Am I?" said the General.

He was interested, he was gratified. He had thought he was eighty. It was a pleasant surprise to find that he was ninety.

'Well, well, well!" he continued. "Ninety . . . it's a good age."

"So we all wish you many happy returns of the day," said Miss Milton.

A chorus of cheers arose. The General looked round the circle of smiling faces. His neighbours . . . his friends . . . his well-wishers . . . He hadn't realised till this moment how much he valued them. They were holding out glasses and singing. The sound was confused and unmelodious. Some of them were singing *For he's a Jolly Good Fellow*, others were singing *Happy Birthday to You*, while yet others were singing *The Boys of the Old Brigade*, but the General didn't mind.

He had been through a trying experience and the shell of crustiness that usually enclosed him had crumbled away. Tears of emotion stood in the dim, red-rimmed eyes.

"Well, sir," said Bill. "How're you feeling? Happy?"

"Happy?" said the General. "I don't think I've felt so happy since—since the Relief of Mafeking."

Chapter 3

Violet Elizabeth Runs Away

"Away from Civilisation," said William scornfully. "It's a dotty subject."

"Ole Frenchie always gives dotty subjects for essays," said Ginger.

"The last one was Wales," said Douglas.

"I wrote a jolly good one on that," said William. "I told about the man that got eaten by one in the Bible and about a dream I once had of one tryin' to get on top of a bus an' endin' up havin' a fight with an octopus. It was a smashin' essay an' he didn't give me a single mark an' he said some jolly nasty things about it."

"He meant the country not the fish," said Henry. "He'd just given a lesson all about it with maps an' things."

"Well, I hadn't been listening," said William in simple explanation.

"Ole Frenchie's against civilisation," said Ginger. "He says he wished he'd lived in the Stone Age."

"I wish he had, too," said William.

"He says that when things get too much for him he

likes to leave the horrors of civilisation behind and make for the peace an' solace of the open countryside."

"Dotty sort of thing he would say," said William.

The four were walking slowly along the road towards the village. William held a bag of sherbet into which they all dipped at intervals, leaving ample traces on their faces and pullovers.

"It's nearly all gone," said William, peering into the bag, "an' it's my turn an' my sherbet, so I'll finish it." He put his head back, held the bag upside down over his face and shook it violently. "Gosh!" he spluttered. "Hardly any of it's gone into my mouth. It's all in my eyes an' nose an' ears."

"Let's lick his face," suggested Douglas.

"No, you won't," said William, dodging their attack. "It's my face an' my sherbet, isn't it, so you can jolly well leave it alone. I can lick it myself if I want to, can't I . . . ? 'Least, I could if my tongue was a bit longer."

They fell to the ground in a struggling heap. Suddenly Ginger's voice cut through the uproar.

"They're comin'! *Quick!*"

The struggling heap disentangled itself and the boys sprang to the side of the road, diving into the dry ditch that ran alongside. At the bend of the road could be seen the crocodile of Rose Mount School. The girls wore the school uniform of navy blue suits and navy blue hats. A tall vague-looking mistress brought up the rear. They straggled along the road then vanished from sight down a narrow lane.

The boys emerged from their hiding-place, looking warily up and down the road.

"She wasn't there, thank goodness!" said William.

"P'raps she's got 'flu," said Henry. "A lot of them have got it."

"My mother had it," said Douglas. "It's called Three Day Flu an' it lasts three weeks."

"I wouldn't mind it lastin' three years if Violet Elizabeth's got it," said William.

Violet Elizabeth Bott was the Outlaw's "pet aversion". She lived at the Hall with her father and mother and attached herself to the Outlaws whenever she found a chance. Her lisp and small angelic face gave an impression of sweetness and docility, but, although only six years old, she was officious and autocratic and overbearing and unreasonable, and the Outlaws had brought their skill in avoiding her to a fine art.

In normal times it had been fairly easy to avoid her, but normal times had suddenly come to an end. Her parents had gone abroad—Mr. Bott on business and Mrs. Bott on a trip to Paris—and they had parked Violet Elizabeth for the time of their absence at Rose Mount School, a select boarding-school for girls on the outskirts of the village. The result was that the situation for the Outlaws was even worse than it had been when she lived at home, for, whenever they met the crocodile of Rose Mount School, Violet Elizabeth would dart out of the ranks to join them, refusing to rejoin the ranks till dragged away, protesting shrilly, by an irate mistress-in-charge. After the first few encounters the Outlaws had kept a watchful eye on their surroundings, prepared to take cover at sight of the Rose Mount crocodile. Violet Elizabeth also kept a watchful eye on her surroundings, obviously ready and eager for the next meeting.

The boys emerged slowly and cautiously from the ditch.

"Thank goodness she wasn't there," said William again, brushing a patch of sherbet off his pullover.

"Out of the jaws of death," said Henry.

"What shall we do now?" said Ginger.

"Let's go to Jenks's farm an' see if he's usin' that new tractor," said William. "I want to see how it works."

But Jenks was not using the new tractor. He was working on his manure heap and chased the boys out of the farmyard with furious flourishes of his stick. William fell into the manure heap and they went to the stream in the wood to wash off the traces. After a somewhat sketchy cleaning process they practised jumping over the stream at its widest point (only Ginger fell in) and swinging across the stream by an overhanging branch till the branch broke and deposited William in midstream, after which they investigated some bubbles which William thought might indicate the presence of a "gas find" but which they finally decided were merely the results of his immersion . . . then made their way back to the old barn.

"Let's have a think about that civilisation essay," said Henry.

"You can do the think," said William. "You're good at that sort of think. You can think out four ideas an' then we can have one each."

"Gosh!" said Ginger, just then. "Who's this?"

A strange figure was coming across the field towards the old barn. It was a short figure dressed in a shapeless trailing coat, the face almost hidden by a thick black mop of hair. They gazed at it in bewilderment as it approached.

"Hello, William!" said a small shrill voice.

"Gosh!" groaned William. "Violet Elizabeth Bott!"

Violet Elizabeth removed the mop-like wig.

"Yeth, ith me, William," she said calmly. "I've run away from thcool."

"Run away?" said William.

"Yeth," said Violet Elizabeth. "I don't like it. Ith a nathty plathe and they give you nathty food. Minthe!" She contorted her small features into a grimace of disgust.

A STRANGE FIGURE WAS COMING ACROSS THE FIELD.

"Minthe twithe in one week. The mithtretheth are nathty too. They're croth all the time."

"But what on earth——?" said William, pointing to the wig that she was now dangling in one hand.

"Ith a dithguithe," said Violet Elizabeth proudly. "I thtole it. Ith a Beatleth wig. It belongth to one of the big girlth and I thtole it for my dithguithe tho that I could run away. And the coat belongth to one of the mithtretheth, I thtole that for my dithguithe, too."

They stared at her helplessly.

"Yes, but what are you goin' to *do*?" said William.

"Thtay with you," said Violet Elizabeth simply. "You mutht hide me tho that they can't find me."

"Well, we *can't*," said William indignantly.

"But you mutht, William," said Violet Elizabeth. "They're nathty people at that thcool. I wouldn't eat minthe and they thaid I muthn't have anything elthe to eat till I'd eaten it, tho I thall thtarve to death if you thend me back." She looked at him appealingly. "You can't thend me back to thtarve to death, William. It would be the thame ath *murdering* me. And if you try to take me back, I'll thcream an' I'll *thcream* . . ."

William turned to the others. His brow was deeply furrowed.

"Gosh! What are we goin' to *do* with her?" he said.

"Take her back," said Ginger.

William gave an ironic snort.

"Yes, screamin' and yellin' all down the road!" he said. "That's a *jolly* good idea, I *mus'* say!"

"She bites, too," said Douglas. "She's got teeth like daggers. She bit me once an' it took *days* to get well."

"It's a sort of moral problem," said Henry slowly.

"What d'you mean, moral problem?" said William.

"Well, she's sort of taken sanctuary with us."

"What's that?" said William.

"Same as a bird sanctuary?" said Douglas.

"Yes, in a way," said Henry, "but it's more *serious* with humans. There were places in the old days where people could take sanctuary—crim'nals an' runaway slaves an' people like that an' as long as they were there no one could get at them."

"Why not?" said William.

" 'Cause the people who kept those places *had* to protect the people who went there an' not let the people they were runnin' away from get at them. It was a—a sort of *moral* duty. I once read a story about it. I think it was in ancient Greek times."

"Well, this isn't ancient Greek times," said William.

"No, but it's the same," said Henry earnestly. "She's come an' asked for sanctuary an' we've got to give it her. It would be *treachery* to hand her over to her enemies. She's—trusted us, you see. She's taken *sanctuary* with us."

They considered this in silence. Violet Elizabeth had lost interest in the discussion and was hopping round the barn on one leg, tripping every now and then over the trailing coat.

"Yes, I s'pose there's somethin' in that," said William at last, "but what can we *do* with her? We can't hide her up for the rest of our lives. We've nowhere to hide her for one thing an' she'd be jolly difficult to hide even if we had. An' she's fussy about food. She'd turn her nose up at any bit of food we could pinch for her. She'd start screamin' an' carryin' on. It'd be as bad as tryin' to hide a ragin' hyena."

"An' we can't take her home," said Ginger. "There's no one there to take her to 'cause her father an' mother's away and there's only workmen there."

"She's a sort of mixture of an orphan an' a refugee," said Douglas. "It makes it jolly difficult."

Violet Elizabeth had joined them, tripping over her coat and falling at William's feet. She sat where she had fallen and adjusted her wig, peering up at them through the tangle of dark hair.

"Ith a lovely dithguithe, ithn't it?" she said.

"Now listen, Violet Elizabeth," said William. "You're a mixture of an orphan an' a refugee, same as Douglas says, an' we can't keep you 'cause we've nowhere to hide you an' we can't take you home 'cause there's no one there 'cause your mother's gone on a trip to Paris."

"The fairground of Europe," said Henry sententiously. "That's what I once heard someone call it."

"Yeth," said Violet Elizabeth with sudden bitterness. "Thee's in Parith, riding on roundabouth and thwinging on thwingth at this fairground and thee dothen't care what happenth to me. Thee juth leaveth me to be *poithoned* by minthe an' thtarved to death. I won't go back to her at all now an' it'll therve her right."

"Well, we can't go on keepin' you for the rest of our lives," said Ginger.

"It would be as bad as that man that had to go about with an albatross tied round his neck," said Henry.

"More like a naggin' hyena tied round our necks," said William. "So you'll *have* to go back, Violet Elizabeth."

Violet Elizabeth glowered at them through the forest of black hair.

"I'm not going to that nathty plathe," she said. Then what could be seen of her face broke into a beaming smile. "I *tell* you what I'll do. I'll get a job. I'd like to get a job."

"What sort of a job?" said William.

"I'll have to think about it," said Violet Elizabeth with maddening uncertainty.

"Well, hurry up," said William. "We've not got all day. What would you like to be?"

"I think I'd like to be a printheth," said Violet Elizabeth.

"Don't be dotty," said William. "You can't get a *job* as a princess."

"I'd like to be a film thtar then," she said at last.

"Well, you couldn't," said William. "It takes *years* to get to be a film star. You might start now eatin' cereals on a commercial, but it'd take *years* to get to be a real film star. An' I bet you'd make a fuss over the cereals."

"Yeth, I'd thpit them out," said Violet Elizabeth placidly. "I don't like therealth. . . . Well, if I can't be a film thtar, I'll ride on a horthe and jump through a hoop.

I thaw a girl doing that onthe and thee wathn't much older than me."

"You can't ride a horse," objected Henry.

"They'd thow me how to," said Violet Elizabeth. "I've theen people doing it. It lookth eathy."

"There isn't a circus anywhere round anyway," said William, "and if there was they wouldn't take you even if you could ride. They'd know who you were and take you home."

"They wouldn't know who I am, William," said Violet Elizabeth. "I'll wear my dithguithe. They couldn't *possibly* know who I am if I wear my dithguithe."

"Anyway, you can't," said Henry firmly.

"Well, I muth do thomething now I'm an orphan," said Violet Elizabeth. "There muth be *thomething* for orphanth to do."

"My mother knew an orphan once," said Douglas. "She helped to get it adopted."

"That'th what I'll do," said Violet Elizabeth with the air of one who has solved a difficult problem to the satisfaction of all concerned. "I'll get mythelf adopted. I'm thick of thcool an' I'm thick of my own mother. Thee goeth off to thith Parith fairground having rideth on roundabouth and thwingth and leaveth me to be poithoned and thtarved to death. I want a nithe new thcool and a nithe new mother, tho you muth get me adopted."

"We can't," said William.

"How could we?" said Henry.

"Put a notith in the potht offith," said Violet Elizabeth. "We got a nithe new gardener that way, tho I might get a nithe new mother that way. Come on. Leth go to the potht offith."

The Outlaws hesitated. The suggestion was fraught with

danger but the present situation was so intolerable that almost any change was welcome.

"Better than jus' stayin' here," whispered William to Ginger. "We'll get rid of her somehow."

They crossed the field to the road and made their way towards the village shops. There were a few passers-by and they threw amused smiles at the shaggy-haired child in the long trailing coat.

"Up to some lark or other," said a genial-looking old man, patting the black wig and withdrawing his hand quickly as Violet uttered a threatening growl.

They reached the post office and stood for a minute outside, examining the notices that were displayed in the window.

"*Home wanted for lovable kitten.*"

"*Young lady wanted to do light household work two mornings a week.*"

"*Spin-drier wanted in exchange for sewing-machine.*"

"They're all written on cardth," said Violet Elizabeth. "You are thtupid not to've brought cardth."

"P'raps she's got cards in the shop," said Douglas.

They entered the post office. It was empty except for the post-mistress, who looked at them without interest or curiosity. The post-mistress was of a philosophic turn of mind. Few things surprised or daunted her.

"Well?" she said. "What can I do for you?"

"We want to put a card in the window," said Violet Elizabeth.

"Where is it?" said the post-mistress.

"We haven't got one," said William.

"If we tell you what we want, will you write it down?" said Violet Elizabeth.

"What is it?" said the post-mistress.

Violet Elizabeth cleared her throat impressively.

THEY STOOD FOR A MINUTE EXAMINING THE NOTICES.

" 'Lovable young lady,' " she said " 'wanth to be adopted by nithe perthon.' "

"All right," said the post-mistress. "Now off you go and no more of your nonsense!"

There was a note of authority in her voice and instinctively they went out of the shop and began to walk down the road.

"We'll go back thoon and thee if thee's found a nithe perthon," said Violet Elizabeth.

"She won't do anything about it, you know," said Henry. "She won't even put the notice up. You've got to pay money to have notices put up and we haven't any."

"An' you've got to put an address," said Ginger, "an'

we can't put the school 'cause you've run away from it an' we can't put your home 'cause there's no one there but the workmen."

"We'll have to think of thomething elthe, then," said Violet Elizabeth.

They had reached the crossroads and stood looking about them uncertainly.

"Well, we can't stay here," said Douglas. "Anyone might come along an' we'd all get into a row . . . Look! Someone's comin' now!"

Mrs. Monks and Miss Caruthers (a middle-aged lady who had recently come to live in the village) were coming down the road, so deep in conversation that they did not notice the group of children clustered there.

"Quick!" said William, diving again into the overgrown ditch. The others followed, crouching behind a spreading tuft of cow parsley. The two women stopped at the crossroads and stood talking. Snatches of their conversation reached the children.

"You see," said Miss Caruthers, "this friend of mine who shall be nameless—I promised not to mention names so I won't. Anyway, this friend of mine wanted to find a little girl to bring up as a companion for her own little girl, who's an only child and needs companionship . . . At last, however, I got in touch with someone who seemed ideal—a widower with a little girl of the right age who wanted to find a suitable home for her with another child . . . I got the interview all fixed up . . . This friend of mine who shall be nameless is staying at the Somerton Arms in Marleigh . . . She's got the Blue Bedroom, you know, that overlooks the rose garden, so charming . . . Anyway, I was going to take the child to the interview this afternoon. She wanted to meet the child alone, you see, so that she could get to know her without a third person being present . . . I was to take the child to the hotel . . . Then I heard by this morning's post that the whole thing has fallen through. The widower's going to marry again and his fiancée's crazy on the child and wants to keep her . . . I meant to run round to the hotel this morning and tell my friend but I've been called to the sick-bed of a dear aunt and have to rush off. I tried to ring my friend up at the hotel but couldn't get through to her . . . I wrote a note for the gardener to take but he's not turned up. I thought I might run across someone else to deliver it but I haven't been successful . . . Well, there's nothing I can do about it, now. So provoking!"

"I'm sorry I can't help," said Mrs. Monks, "but the Women's Guild committee is waiting for me and I'm late already."

"Oh, well," said Miss Caruthers with a sigh, "it's just one of those things, I suppose."

"Yes," agreed Mrs. Monks sympathetically, "it's just one of those things . . . And I must really go now. Good-bye for the present."

She set off hurriedly down the road in the direction of the Village Hall.

Miss Caruthers stood irresolute for a moment . . . Suddenly she brightened. She had caught sight of a boy's head in the ditch.

"Boy!" she called.

It was William who, impelled by curiosity, had inadvertently raised his head above the jungle of grass and cow parsley. Slowly, reluctantly, he emerged and approached her.

Miss Caruthers had not lived in the neighbourhood long enough to distinguish one boy from another. William's face wore its most ferocious scowl and somehow the scowl made him look earnest and reliable and conscientious.

Here was a boy, she felt, who could be trusted and depended on.

"Will you do something for me, boy?" she said.

"Uh-huh," said William guardedly.

Miss Caruthers took a note from her handbag.

"Will you go to the Somerton Arms at Marleigh and deliver this note for me? . . . Here's sixpence for your trouble."

William crammed the note into his pocket without looking at it and received the sixpence into a grubby palm.

"Thanks," he said, "but——"

He was about to explain that his time was fully occupied for the present and that he could not deliver the note till later when he found that Miss Caruthers had turned away and was already scurrying off in the direction of the bus stop.

The other four climbed out of the ditch.

"Thatth what I want to be," said Violet Elizabeth, beaming joyfully. "I want to be the little girl'th companion. I'd *like* to be the little girl'th companion. I'll have a nithe new friend an' a nithe new mother. Ith juth what I want. The'll be waiting for me now and the'll never know I'm not the real one. Come on. Leth go to Marleigh quick."

They stared at her, dismayed and bewildered. It was William who pointed out the one bright spot in the situation.

"It's a way of gettin' rid of her," he said. "We can jus' take her there an' leave her." He opened his hand. "Look! She gave me sixpence."

"You mutht buy me a lolly then," said Violet Elizabeth, "to thtop me thtarving to death."

"All right," said William slowly. "If we buy you a lolly, will you promise to go back to school straight away?"

"I'll think about it," said Violet Elizabeth graciously.

Ginger ran back to the shops and returned with a lollipop.

"Now will you go back to school?" said William, handing it to her.

"No," said Violet Elizabeth, "I thaid I'd think about it and I've thought about it and I've dethided not to."

"Gosh!" groaned William. "It looks as if we've got her hung round our necks for the rest of our lives."

Violet Elizabeth had dropped her lollipop on to the road, but she picked it up and with dainty movements of her small red tongue proceeded to lick the dust off it.

"*Look* at her!" said Ginger. "Turns up her nose at mince an' eats dust!"

"I don't mind the tathte of dutht," said Violet Elizabeth. "Ith quite *clean* dutht . . . And I made up all that about the minthe. I wanted to run away from thcool tho I made all that up about the minthe to give me a reathon for running away. It wath clever of me, wathn't it?"

"You're a story-teller," said Douglas sternly.

"I know I am," said Violet Elizabeth with an air of modest pride. "I'm a very *good* thtory-teller."

"Oh, come on," said William disgustedly. "Let's take her to that place an' drop her there and get rid of her."

"If we ever can!" said Douglas with an ironic laugh.

They trailed over the fields to Marleigh. The Somerton Arms was a picturesque old-fashioned hotel that stood back from the road in a picturesque old-fashioned garden.

They stood at the gate for a moment or two, considering it.

"I'm going to have a nithe new mother," said Violet Elizabeth complacently. "My own mother dothn't care for anything but riding on roundabouth in Parith, tho I don't want her any more."

* * *

Mrs. Bott was not riding on roundabouts in Paris. She was sitting in her bedroom at the Somerton Arms, dressed up to the nines, awaiting her visitor. During the last few months Mrs. Bott had been planning fresh manœuvres to force her way into the ranks of the local aristocracy. She had faced the fact that she was not aristocratic and she longed with all her soul to be aristocratic. The aristocracy had been to Paris. They referred to it as casually as if it had been Hadley. They came back with Paris outfits and Paris hats. Mrs. Bott had never been to Paris, had never worn a Paris outfit or a Paris hat . . . and the urge to do these things became so irresistible that, when Mr. Bott went to Holland on business and workmen had taken possession of the Hall (Mrs. Bott had all her rooms redecorated regularly with every changing fashion), she decided to seize the opportunity and go to Paris. She had gone to Paris. She had gone to Paris and she failed to understand what the aristocracy saw in Paris. She had been bored and bewildered in Paris and her thoughts had turned more and more frequently to Violet Elizabeth at Rose Mount School. To judge from her letters, Violet Elizabeth was not happy at Rose Mount School, but Violet Elizabeth was seldom happy anywhere for long . . . Violet Elizabeth demanded constant change and excitement and if no one else would provide them she generally managed to provide them herself.

Wandering through the Paris shops, sitting dejectedly in the Luxembourg Gardens, gazing vacantly at the pictures in the Louvre, Mrs. Bott thought about Violet Elizabeth, and she came to the conclusion that the root of the trouble was the fact that Violet Elizabeth was an only child. What Violet Elizabeth needed was a little companion. Her mind's eye saw Violet Elizabeth, under the influence of the little companion, transformed into a

quiet, good-tempered, obedient child, and she embarked
on the process of finding the little companion. She decided
to move secretly so as not to set the village tongues wag-
ging, as the village tongues were apt to wag on the slight-
est provocation. She wrote to Miss Caruthers because
Miss Caruthers was a new-comer to the village who had
as yet made few friends and could be trusted not to spread
the news. She decided to leave Paris at once without
waiting for her husband's return or the completion of the
decorations at the Hall. She felt that she couldn't endure
Paris a day longer. It was full of noise and confusion and
people who didn't understand English. She had decided
to come home incognito, as it were, and stay quietly at
the Somerton Arms till her husband had returned and the
decorations at the Hall were completed.

Then she would blossom forth in all her Paris glory and
send out invitations to the local aristocracy for a party
that would put in the shade every other party ever held
in the neighbourhood. She had not forgotten the Paris
glory. She had spent her last few days in Paris acquiring
it. She had had things done to her face and she had had
things done to her hair. When they'd finished with her
face, her eyes—blue shadowed and heavily lashed—
seemed to leave no room for the rest of her features, and
when they'd finished with her hair she looked as if she
hadn't got any. She had bought a Paris dress and a Paris
hat. The Paris dress was too short and tight for her dumpy
little figure, but the assistant said that it was what people
were wearing, so Mrs. Bott decided to wear it. The assistant who sold her the Paris hat said it was a dream, but
Mrs. Bott couldn't help thinking it was more like a nightmare. The assistant said that it suggested the latest trend
of fashionable taste, but to Mrs. Bott it suggested nothing
so much as the Eiffel Tower rising from the middle of a

frying-pan. Again the assistant said that it was what people were wearing and again Mrs. Bott steeled herself to wear it. She was wearing both hat and dress now as she sat in her bedroom in the Somerton Arms awaiting the little companion. She was wearing them partly to get used to them and partly because she wanted to impress the little companion as a woman of rank and fashion who moved in high aristocratic circles.

She was just wondering whether she'd got her hat on back to front when there came a knock at the door and Mrs. Kennal, the manageress of the hotel, entered closing the door behind her. She looked pale and shaken.

"There's a child," she said. "At least I think it's a child. Something about you expecting her . . ."

"Oh yes," said Mrs. Bott, moving the hat sideways. "I'm expecting her. Show her in."

Mrs. Kennal opened the door and a small figure entered. The wig hid the face completely and the lollipop dangled from it, inextricably entangled in the thick black hair. The coat followed like a bedraggled tail. Mrs. Bott gave an hysterical scream.

"Go away, you horrible child!" she cried. "I wouldn't let you *near* my Violet Elizabeth. Go *away*! I wouldn't let my Violet Elizabeth *see* you even. It would *kill* her, the sweet sensitive little love! She couldn't bear the *sight* of you. Go AWAY!"

But, at the same moment, Violet Elizabeth had also given an hysterical scream.

"I don't *want* you for my mother, you nathty woman!" Her voice rose in a prolonged wail. "I want my own nithe mother. I want my own Mummy. Go away, you nathty horrid woman! If you don't go away I'll thcream and I'll thcream and I'll *thcream* . . ."

Mrs. Bott stared at her. The voice was familiar. The

MRS. BOTT GAVE AN HYSTERICAL SCREAM.

scream was familiar. The wig had dropped off revealing a small distorted face that was familiar.

"Oh, my darling!" she said, throwing herself on the floor beside Violet Elizabeth.

"Go away!" screamed Violet Elizabeth again.

But Mrs. Bott's abrupt descent had displaced the Paris hat, disarranged the Paris hair-do and reduced her almost to her old self.

"Oh, *Mummy!*" said Violet Elizabeth. "My own *nithe* Mummy!"

They sat on the floor, clasped in each other's arms.

And then Miss Golightly entered. She had tracked her errant pupil to the Somerton Arms and was not in the best of tempers.

Mrs. Bott rose to her feet.

"Miss Golightly," she said sternly, "you have a lot to explain."

Miss Golightly had a lot to explain and she explained it. The 'flu epidemic had reduced the staff to half its normal numbers and things had, she admitted, got a little out of hand. But that a pupil of Rose Mount School should run away was unprecedented, unthinkable. She fixed a stony gaze on Violet Elizabeth.

"And *you*, Violet Elizabeth," she said, "have something to explain. Kindly explain it."

Violet Elizabeth turned her eyes from one to the other. Her small sweet face wore a look of troubled innocence.

"It wathn't my fault," she said plaintively. "It wath thothe horrid boyth. They made me do it."

"What boys?" said Miss Golightly.

Mrs. Kennal had joined the group in the bedroom.

"There were four boys at the door . . ." she said.

But the four boys were at the door no longer. They had heard fragments of the conversation and they were

following Mr. French's example . . . leaving the horrors
of civilisation behind them and making for the peace and
solace of the open countryside.

Chapter 4

William Brown, Hero

William walked slowly along the road towards Ginger's house. He did not see the fields and hedges and houses that bordered the road. He saw only a quay crowded with people, heard only their deafening cheers as he guided his yacht skilfully into position.

He was returning from a lone voyage round the world . . . through the Doldrums, the Roaring Forties, the Bass Strait, the Horn. He had been buffeted by ferocious storms, lifted high in the air and plunged deep into the trough, his cabin and the whole boat flooded time and time again, his radio and self-steering gear put out of action, vital parts of his equipment swept into the sea. But now, after breath-taking adventure, he had reached home.

The Mayor and Corporation were assembled on the quay. William stepped ashore to receive their congratulations. The cheers rose to a note of thunder. A Court Official made his way through the crowd and handed an envelope to William. William opened it. It contained a summons to Buckingham Palace. He . . .

"Hello, William!"

William stopped, realising that he had reached the gate of Ginger's house.

"Hello," he said, tearing himself reluctantly away from the crowded quay.

Ginger joined him in the road.

"I say!" he said. There was a note of subdued excitement in his voice. "My aunt's been to lunch with us an'—d'you know what?"

"No," said William.

"Well, she kept on an' on about doin' service to the community . . ."

"What's the community?" said William a little irritably, as he watched the Court Official fade into the distance.

"It's people," said Ginger earnestly. "It's anyone. Helpin' the community means helpin' people. Anyone. An' this aunt of mine promised me ten shillings if I did somethin' to help the community."

"Oh," said William. "That'd be jolly useful. We could do a lot with ten shillin's . . . What sort of things did she mean?"

"Well, she kept talkin' about things that people had done for the community, like puttin' a stop to slavery an' settin' up the Health Service an' stoppin' people gettin' executed in public."

"It's too late to do any of those," said William after a moment's thought. "They've been done."

"But there's lots of other things left," said Ginger. "Little things like—like visitin' people in hospital."

"I tried that once," said William. "I once went to see a cousin of my mother's in hospital an' there was a wheel-chair in the corridor an' I got into it 'cause I wanted to see if I could start it an' I could an' then I couldn't stop it . . . They made an awful fuss. They wouldn't even let me see this cousin of my mother's. They jus' turned me out without even listenin' to me." His sense of grievance rose afresh. "I bet they could have got that trolley full of stuff out of the way in time if they'd tried."

"Then there was doin' errands for old people," said Ginger.

"I've tried that too," said William. "My mother made me go shoppin' for old Miss Hopkins when she'd got 'flu an' she gave me a shoppin'-list an' she's got such awful writin' that I couldn't read it. I thought she'd put down 'pear soup' an' it turned out to be 'Pear's Soap' an' I'd been to nearly every grocer in Hadley askin' for pear soup an' they'd been jolly rude to me an' she was jolly rude to me too when I got back, an' if that's all this aunt of yours can tell you about servin' the community, I've had about enough of it."

"No, there were other things," said Ginger. "She told us about some children that went round sweepin' snow away for old age pensioners."

William looked round the sleepy summer landscape.

"All right," he said with heavy sarcasm, "you find the snow an' I'll sweep it away."

"But there were lots more things she said," persisted Ginger. "She's got a friend that works at a Citizens' Advice Bureau."

"What's that?" said William.

"It's—well, it's sort of advisin' citizens," said Ginger uncertainly.

"What about?" said William.

"Anythin'," said Ginger. "They come an' ask you to— well, to advise 'em, an'—an', well, you advise 'em."

"Is that all?" said William.

"I think so," said Ginger.

"Sounds easy enough," said William. There was a new note of interest in his voice. "Gosh, I could do *that* all right. I bet I could advise anyone about anythin'—where do they do it?"

"I think they've got a sort of office," said Ginger.

"We can manage that all right, too," said William.

"The old barn makes a smashin' office . . . an' they jus' come an' ask advice an' you give it 'em?"

"I think so," said Ginger again.

Things moved so quickly when William took charge of them that it always left Ginger feeling slightly bewildered.

"It's a jolly easy way of earnin' ten shillin's," said William. "How much do they pay for it?"

"Nothin'," said Ginger, " 'cause it's a service to the community."

"Oh, well, we'll get the ten shillin's in the end," said William, "so that doesn't matter. Come on. Let's put up a notice an' get started."

Ginger found a large envelope that had contained a gardening catalogue in a waste-paper basket at home, and William slowly and laboriously wrote the notice on the back:

CITTISENS ADVISE BURRO

Together they fixed it on the door of the old barn and stood in the doorway awaiting clients.

"You know, we've tried things like this before," said Ginger uneasily, "an' they didn't come off."

"Some of them didn't," admitted William, "but I bet this one will. Well, it couldn't go wrong, could it? I mean, anyone can give advice. It's a jolly easy way of earnin' money."

"They might ask us things we don't know about," said Ginger.

"Oh, I know about most things," said William airily, "an' I can make 'em up if I don't."

"Look!" said Ginger. "Someone's comin' . . . It's Anthea Green."

Anthea Green was making her way slowly across the field. Anthea was a child of about William's age with dark hair, dark eyes, a wistful expression and an indomitable will.

"It would be her," said William gloomily.

Anthea paused at the door, read the notice and entered.

"You've spelt it wrong," she said.

"There's different ways of spellin' things," said William with dignity, "an' my way's as good as anyone else's."

"Oh, all right," said Anthea. "What do you charge for it?"

"Nothin'," said William. "It's a service to the community."

"What's that?" said Anthea.

"People," said William. "It means helpin' people."

"You mean you've got to help anyone that's in trouble for nothing?"

"I s'pose so," said William, a little doubtfully.

"Well, I'm in trouble," said Anthea, "so you'll have to help me."

"We—we'll give you advice," said William.

"You said you'd *help*," said Anthea accusingly. "First you say you'll help and then you say you won't. You're a story-teller an' a cheat an' . . ."

"Oh, all right," said William. "What d'you want anyway?"

"A new fancy dress costume," said Anthea calmly.

"A what?" said William.

"A new fancy dress costume," repeated Anthea. "Maisie Fellowes is having a fancy dress party tonight for her birthday an' I've only got a silly old Austrian peasant girl's costume that I've worn and everyone *knows* an' my mother says she won't get me another one, an' I won't *go* without another one."

" 'Course we can't get you a new fancy dress costume," said William. "Citizens' Advice Bureaux aren't there to get people new fancy dress costumes. They jus' give advice. Now listen. I'll give you some advice. I . . ."

"You said *help*," said Anthea. She stamped her foot angrily. "You *promised*. You said you helped the community an' you said the community was people so I'm the community 'cause I'm a *person*, aren't I?"

"But we can't get you a fancy dress costume," said William. "How can we?"

Anthea changed her tactics. She gave a high-pitched sarcastic laugh.

" 'Course you can't," she said. "You're just a silly little boy. You go about boasting you can do things an' you can't do anything but boast."

"Oh, can't I?" said William. He felt himself lifted suddenly on an enormous wave. Water flooded the cabin, flooded the whole boat. He fought furiously to take in sail, secure the tiller lines and pump out the water at the same time . . . "Huh! I've done things that not many people in the world've done."

"Have you really!" sneered Anthea. "Funny that you can't get me a new fancy dress costume then!"

" 'Course I can," said William, releasing his hold on the tiller lines. " *'Course* I can!"

The words were out of his mouth before he realised that he had said them.

"Now you've promised," said Anthea triumphantly. "You've *promised* so you'll have to do it. If you break a promise you're a liar and a cheat."

"Here! Wait a minute!" said William.

But Anthea knew when to beat a retreat. Having gained an advantage she didn't intend to forfeit it by further parley.

They watched her trim little figure trotting back across the field to the road.

"Well, you've done it now," said Ginger.

"What?" said William.

"Promised," said Ginger, "an' she'll never let you off."

"Oh well," said William with an attempt at non-chalance. "I bet I can do it all right."

"Find a new fancy dress for her?" said Ginger. "How?"

"Give me time to think, can't you?" said William test-ily. "Anyway it's lunch-time an' I'm jolly hungry. I 'spect I'll have thought of a way all right when I've had some food."

Ginger gave an ironical snort.

"It'll take more than a bit of food to get us out of *this*," he said.

William found Ginger waiting at his gate after lunch.

"Well," said Ginger, "thought of a way?"

"Stop fussin' about it," said William. "I bet I'll find a way all right if only you'll leave me alone. Come on, let's go down to the village. We might find somethin' in the village."

"An' we might not," said Ginger with a mirthless laugh.

"Oh shut up!" said William.

They slowly walked on down the road to the village. Outside the Village Hall a large notice proclaimed JUMBLE SALE and streams of women were entering and emerging from the doorway.

"Come on in," said William. "We might find somethin' in a jumble sale. You never know."

"You gen'rally know you won't," said Ginger, repeat-ing the mirthless laugh.

"Oh, come on in," said William.

They entered the Village Hall. Stalls of battered house-hold goods, battered sports equipment, clothes . . .

"*Look!*" said William.

For there, prominently displayed on clothes-hangers, at the back of a stall presided over by Miss Milton and

"GOSH!" SAID WILLIAM. "THAT ONE LOOKS ALL RIGHT."

Miss Thompson, hung two obviously fancy dress costumes. One consisted of a full flowered skirt, black laced
velvet bodice, and white short-sleeved muslin blouse, the
other of lederhosen with embroidered braces and shorts.

"Gosh!" said William. "That one looks all right. The
girl's one. It's a fancy dress costume all right. How much
money have we got?"

"I've got eightpence," said Ginger.

"An' I've got sixpence halfpenny," said William.

"That makes one an' twopence halfpenny," said Ginger
after a few moments' silent calculation.

"I bet it won't cost all that much," said William. "It'll probably be about sixpence. Come on, let's ask."

He approached Miss Milton, twisting his homely features into their ingratiating smile.

" 'Scuse me," he said. "Are those—are they fancy dress costumes?"

"Yes, dear," said Miss Milton, moving a china jug into a position that concealed the broken handle. "They're Hansel and Gretel—the characters from that delightful fairy story of Grimm, you know."

"We only want the girl's one," said William.

"It seems a pity to separate them," said Miss Milton, trying the effect of an artificial poppy on the brim of Mrs. Monks's last year's hat . . . and deciding against it.

"They make such a delightful couple, but you can have the Gretel costume for four and six if you like."

"Four an' six!" squeaked William indignantly. "We haven't got all *that* money!"

"Perhaps we could reduce it a little," said Miss Thompson.

"Certainly not," said Miss Milton. "It's a beautiful costume. Very well made and in excellent condition."

"Listen," said William earnestly. "We'll give you one an' twopence halfpenny for it."

"Certainly not," said Miss Milton again. "Now don't stand there blocking people's way. Buy the costume if you want it and go away if you don't."

William and Ginger went slowly out into the road.

"Well, that settles it," said Ginger. "We'll jus' have to give up that ten shillin's now."

"No, we won't," said William grimly.

It was not the thought of the ten shillings that brought the note of resolution into his voice. It was the vision of Anthea's face upraised to him in gratitude and admiration. She had called him a "silly little boy". She had said that he could do nothing but boast. She must see him as he really was.

"But we've not *got* four an' six," said Ginger.

"Well, we can *get* it, can't we?" said William.

"How?" said Ginger. "We've only got one an' two-pence halfpenny. We'd have to get"—he wrestled with the sum for some moments—"three an' fourpence halfpenny . . . Well, jus' tell me how to get three an' fourpence halfpenny out of nothin' an' nowhere."

"All right, I will when I've thought of it," said William.

"We've tried *hundreds* of ways of gettin' money," said Ginger, "an' none of them have ever come off. We'll have to give it up. It's jus' "—remembering a phrase of his mother's—"one of those days."

"Oh is it?" said William. "Well, I'm not goin' to let it be one of them!"

Victor Jameson was approaching, walking jauntily down the road, swinging a plastic bucket in one hand. He stopped when he met them.

"Hello," he said. "What're you doin'?"

"Nothin'," said William morosely. "What are you?"

"Nothin' jus' now," said Victor, "but I've been workin' jolly hard."

"What at?" said Ginger.

"Earnin' money," said Victor.

"Oh," said William.

"Where?" said Ginger.

"How?" said William.

"Clearin' up litter at The Towers—Mr. Monson's place at Mellings you know," said Victor. "They had a fête in the big meadow on Saturday an' the people that went to it left a lot of litter an' Mr. Monson's been payin' us threepence a bucketful for clearin' it up. I've been there all mornin' an' I've earned four an' six."

"Four an' *six*!" said William. He turned to Ginger. "Come on."

"What about the bucket?" said Ginger.

"You can borrow mine," said Victor. "It'll save me the trouble of carryin' it home."

"Thanks," said William.

They took the bucket and set off across the fields.

"We'd better hurry," said William. "There's no time to lose. The fancy dress party's tonight."

("Oh, William, you are wonderful," she would say. "I *knew* you'd do it." And he would give his nonchalant shrug and reply, "Oh, when I say I'll do things, I gen'rally do them, you know.")

They relaxed their pace as they neared The Towers. A large meadow stretched on either side of it.

"Well, it's not this one," said William surveying the unbroken stretch of grass. "Let's go on to the other."

They passed the large iron entrance gates and stood gazing through the hedge on the other side.

"That one's cleared up too," said Ginger.

"No, it isn't," said William. "Look! You can see a lot of little wooden pegs in the grass. I bet they were put there to mark out stalls an' competitions an' things, an' the people that cleared up the litter didn't bother to clear them up. Let's clear them up. I bet he'll pay us a special high price for it 'cause it's—well, it's skilled labour, bendin' down an' pullin' them all out of the ground sep'rately . . . Come on."

They scraped through the hedge into the meadow and set to work, pulling the small wooden pegs out of the ground and putting them into the bucket. It was just as they were pulling up the last one that they saw the tall, heavily built man approaching.

"It's Mr. Monson," said William. "He'll be jolly grateful."

As the man came nearer they saw that his face was congested with anger, his bushy brows set in a ferocious scowl.

"He doesn't look grateful," said Ginger.

"What d'you mean by trespassing on my property?" roared Mr. Monson.

"We're clearing up litter from the fête," explained William.

"Litter?" said Mr. Monson. "The fête was in the meadow on the other side of the house and the litter was cleared up hours ago."

"It *couldn't* have been," said William triumphantly, " 'cause we've found a jolly lot of it. We've found all these little pegs that were used to mark out stalls an' things an' we've pulled 'em all up. They'd have been trippin' people up all over the place or else some sheep'd've eaten 'em in mistake for grass an' choked to death. You ought to pay us more than threepence a bucket 'cause it's skilled labour."

Mr. Monson looked into the bucket and gave a bellow of rage.

"Are you aware, you crazy young fools," he said, "that on the very eve of an important archaeological excavation you have destroyed all the landmarks that have been carefully set out?"

"Yes, but——" began William.

"Are you aware," said Mr. Monson, "that the space between each of those pegs has been carefully measured out to mark the position of our grid, that you've wasted *days*, *weeks* of work, that our volunteer workers are arriving tomorrow and that we shall have to start again at the very beginning of our preparations?"

"Well, we'll help," said William. "I've got a ruler at home. We'll measure it all out for you again an' we'll only

MR. MONSON'S FACE WAS CONGESTED WITH ANGER.

charge you three an' fourpence halfpenny for it an'——"

Mr. Monson advanced upon them and as he advanced his form seemed to assume enormous proportions, his face seemed to grow dark and massive and ogre-like. He seized the bucket, emptied the pegs on to the ground and flung the bucket at William's head.

"Get out!" he thundered. "Get OUT!"

Swiftly and silently William and Ginger got out, snatching up the bucket, scrambling through the hedge, running down the road and not stopping for breath till they had put a safe distance between themselves and the stately edifice of The Towers.

"Well, I've never seen anyone as mad as that," said Ginger.

"An' I bet they weren't really archaeological stuff," said William. "I shouldn't be s'prised if they didn't mark somewhere where he's hid somethin' that he didn't want people to know about."

"He was cert'nly up to no good," agreed Ginger. "You could tell that."

"Like that train robb'ry where they got millions of pounds. Well, they'd got to hide it somewhere. They couldn't put it all in their Post Office Savin's or the Post Office'd get suspicious. I bet all these volunteer diggers he talked about were members of the gang in disguise comin' to hide the loot an' the little pegs were to show where they'd hid it."

"Well, we scared him all right," said Ginger.

"We cert'nly did," said William.

Their self-respect partially restored, they crossed the stile into the field and made their way slowly homewards.

"We're not much nearer that four an' sixpence," said William.

"No, we're not," said Ginger. "It jus' goes on an' on bein' one of those days."

"That Citizen's Advice Bureau idea's not much good," said William. "I can't think how this friend of your aunt's sticks it."

"Well, we'll jus' have to give it up," said Ginger.

"No, it might turn out all right," said William. The vision of Anthea's face, alight with joy and gratitude, still hovered at the back of his mind. "Let's go an' have another look at the jumble sale."

Pausing only to throw the bucket into Victor Jameson's garden, they returned to the Village Hall.

The jumble sale was still in full swing. Miss Milton's stall was considerably depleted, but the fancy dress costumes of Hansel and Gretel still hung at the back. There was no sign of Miss Milton. Miss Thompson presided over the stall alone. She saw William and Ginger in the doorway and came down to them.

"Miss Milton's gone to see about the tea," she said with a conspiratorial smile, "and she's left me in charge. I really don't see why you shouldn't have the Gretel dress you wanted. I don't think that anyone else is going to buy it. Much better let it go at a reduced price than have it left on our hands. How much did you say you'd give for it?"

"One an' twopence halfpenny," said William. "We tried to get a bit more but somethin' went wrong."

"Well, I don't see why I shouldn't let you have it for that," said Miss Thompson. "Come along in and I'll make it into a nice parcel for you."

"Thanks *awfully*," said William.

They followed her to the stall and she began to pack the costume into a paper carrier, chattering volubly.

"The two costumes didn't really come together. They came separately and it was Miss Milton's idea to put them together as Hansel and Gretel. She thought they'd sell better that way, but really I think they'd have sold better separately. Anyway, I want to get the stall cleared as quickly as I can, so here it is."

William and Ginger dug into their pockets and brought out the one and twopence halfpenny.

"Splendid!" said Miss Thompson. "Carry it carefully, now. We don't want to get it crushed and——"

But William and Ginger were already at the doorway.

"Well, *somethin*'s turned out all right at last," said William as they set off along the road. "Come on. Let's take it to her quick."

"Funny sort of service to the community when you come to think of it," said Ginger.

"It's a jolly good one," said William. "It's worth more than ten shillin's. We've taken more than ten shillin's worth of trouble over it, anyway."

"I hope my aunt'll look at it like that," said Ginger.

"Anthea'll be grateful," said William.

There was a fatuous smile on his lips. He shrugged his shoulders and gesticulated as he walked along the road. ("Well, you wanted a fancy dress, so I got you a fancy dress. That's all there is to it . . . No trouble at all. Only took a minute or two. Oh no, I'm not all that wonderful. It's jus' that when I say I'll do a thing I do it. I'm jus' made that way that's all . . .")

"Here we are," said Ginger, "an' look! She's in the garden."

They stopped at Anthea's gate. Anthea came running across the lawn to them. Her eyes lit up with eagerness and she clasped her hands joyfully when she saw the paper carrier.

"Oh, you've got one!" she said. "You've *got* one!"

"Oh, yes," said William nonchalantly. "We've got one all right."

"OH, YOU'VE GOT ONE!" SAID ANTHEA.

She prattled excitedly as William fumbled with the
fastening of the carrier.

"I knew you'd get it, William. I *knew* you would! I'd
have *died* if I'd had to wear that horrible old thing again."
She gave a mischievous little laugh. "Do you know what
I did jus' to make *sure* that I wouldn't have to wear it? I
took it down to the jumble sale this morning. I *knew*
you'd get me a new one, William, but I wanted to see
the very, *very* last of the hateful old one. Miss Milton put
it on her stall and it'll have gone for ever by now, thank
goodness . . . Oh, *do* show me the new one, William.
Quickly! Quickly! I can't wait . . ."

The smile froze on her lips as William drew the Gretel costume from the paper carrier.

"It's the *old* one," she screamed. "It's the wretched *old* one. You beastly beastly *beasts*! You've brought back the old one . . . I'll never forgive you all my life. I *hate* you, you horrible *beasts*! You——"

She stopped, choking with rage, gathering her breath for another outburst. Her cheeks were red with anger. There was a tigerish gleam in her eyes.

It was Ginger who first turned to flee and instinctively William followed him. They ran till they were out of sight of Anthea's house then walked on for a few moments in silence.

"Well, it's not stopped bein' one of those days, not for a single second, has it?" said Ginger.

"No," agreed William.

"An' we're not likely to get that ten shillin's from my aunt now, so we're left without a penny in the world."

"Yes," agreed William, "an—gosh! What a girl! More like a monster than a yuman bein'."

"She might have been a *bit* grateful after all the trouble we took," said Ginger. "I didn't know she was like that."

"They're all like that when you get to know 'em," said William.

"Everyone seems to've been against us today, right from the very beginnin'," said Ginger.

"Yes," said William, "an' there's nothin' we can do about it."

"No," said Ginger, "there's nothin' left to do but jus' go home."

"Yes," said William. "I've had jus' about enough of everythin' for one day."

"Yes," said Ginger, "so've I."

They parted at Ginger's gate.

William proceeded slowly down the road towards his home. His mind went back over the events of the day . . . the thundering rage of Mr. Monson, the angry scorn of Anthea, the ignominious flight from Mr. Monson, the still more ignominious flight from Anthea . . . and for a moment or two a sense of failure possessed his spirit. But only for a moment or two. William's spirit could not harbour a sense of failure for long. Again he reviewed the events of the day . . . and dismissed them. They belonged to the world of fantasy, dreamlike, unreal. With relief he turned to the world of reality.

Thunders of applause arose from the crowd as his car turned in at the gates of Buckingham Palace.

The doors were flung open. Bowing flunkeys escorted him into the Royal presence. The Royal family stood round, smiling at him in admiration and gratitude, proud of the honour and renown he had brought to the country.

The applause from the crowd outside seemed to shake the very ground on which he stood.

He knelt on the velvet cushion.

The sword lightly touched his shoulder.

"Arise, Sir William Brown!"

Chapter 5

William's Adventure Society

"What's that thing he said we hadn't got any of?" said William.

"Initiative," said Henry.

"Oh . . ." said William. "What is it?"

"Doin' things without bein' told to," said Henry.

"Gosh!" said William in surprise. "Seems to me we're always doin' that. What were the other things he said we hadn't got any of?"

"Enterprise," said Ginger.

"Self-reliance," said Douglas.

"So he said we'd got to have societies," said Henry.

"Oh, was that what he was talkin' about?" said William. "I thought he was talkin' about takin' an interest in world affairs an' not jumpin' over his tulip bed."

"He began with those," said Henry, "an' then he went on to societies."

"Well, I didn't hear much of that last part," said William. "Victor Jameson was tryin' to get a match-box out of my pocket an' I was tryin' to stop him. It began with me gettin' it out of his . . . What did he say about societies?"

"He said we'd got to have 'em," said Ginger.

"Start 'em on our own an' run 'em on our own," said Henry.

The headmaster had given a pep talk to the boys that morning. He had said that all the school societies had been organised by the staff and were run by the staff, supported only half-heartedly by the pupils. He urged the boys to form societies on their own, to organise them and run them and put some real hard work and enthusiasm into them. He added, as a hasty afterthought, that they must obtain their form master's permission for any society they decided to form.

"It's not a bad idea," said William thoughtfully.

It happened that time was hanging rather heavy on his hands. This didn't often happen but when it did he generally took steps to remedy it.

"Yes, it's not a bad idea at all," he said. "I don't see why we shouldn't start one."

"D'you mean stamps or stars or rocks an' things?" said Ginger. "They've got all those already."

"Gosh, no! Not *that* sort!" said William contemptuously. "We'll think of somethin' a bit more excitin' than that!"

"He said that modern youth has lost all sense of adventure," said Henry.

"That's what we'll have, then," said William. "We'll show him we've not. We'll have an Adventure Society."

"What'll we do in it?" said Douglas.

"Adventures," said William simply.

They considered this in silence for a moment or two.

"He said we'd got to have the permission of the form master," said Ginger.

"All right, we'll get it," said William. "Ole Frenchie can't stop us if the headmaster says we ought to. It would be *mutiny*."

"I wouldn't put mutiny past ole Frenchie," said Ginger darkly.

"Anyway, we can try him," said Henry. "Let's catch him after school today."

"Yes," agreed William, "an' I'll be extra polite to put him in a good mood."

They caught Mr. French after school. His small tight face wore its usual grim expression. He looked at them suspiciously as they approached.

"Well, well, well," he said. "What is it?"

"Please, sir," said William, baring his teeth in his glassy smile, "can we start a society?"

"A what?" snapped Mr. French, ignoring the glassy smile.

"Society," said William, "same as ole—I mean, same as the headmaster says we ought to, showin' "—he turned to Henry—"what was it?"

"Initiative," said Henry.

"Yes, that an'—an' the other things he said."

The tenseness of Mr. French's expression did not relax.

"What sort of a society?" he said.

"Adventure Society," said William.

Mr. French's features shot fiercely together.

"Certainly not," he said. "Your entire existence seems to consist of a series of highly deplorable adventures and I shall certainly not countenance any extension of your activities."

"But, please, sir," said William, "we're only tryin' to do what the headmaster told us to. That's the only reason why we want to start this society 'cause the headmaster *told* us to, so we—we sort of feel it's our *duty*."

"PLEASE, SIR," SAID WILLIAM, "CAN WE START A SOCIETY?"

"A matter of conscience, sir," said Henry.

The grimace of Mr. French's features gave place to a sardonic smile.

"I suggest a Nature Study Society, then, or a Bird Watching Society. Both are quiet, seemly activities and would, I am sure, satisfy the tenderest of consciences. I'm glad to find you so eager to please your instructors and hope to see some reflection of it in your next homework. Good-bye."

They watched him gloomily as he strode out of the school door and down the drive.

"Sarcastic," said Henry.

"Batty," said Ginger.

"Inyuman," said William.

"Anarchist," said Douglas a little uncertainly. He'd come across the word in a book the day before and wasn't quite sure what it meant.

"Well, what shall we do now?" said Ginger.

"We might try bird-watching," said Douglas tentatively. "They do it on television. Building nests an' singin' and layin' eggs. Eatin' stuff off bird tables."

"Gosh! I'm not goin' to watch birds," said William. "They never do anythin' interestin'. I'd sooner watch rats if I've got to watch an animal."

"We could watch rats you know," said Ginger. "They're takin' down that old stable nex' to Frankie Parson's house to build a bungalow an' there's any amount of rats there. He says you can see 'em runnin' about all over the place."

"No," said William doggedly. "I'm goin' to have this Adventure Society. If ole Frenchie won't give us permission we'll jolly well do it without." He was silent for a moment then continued thoughtfully, "Can't think why he wouldn't let us. Got mad about it all of a sudden. He didn't give any reason. Seemed sort of as if he was scared of us startin' it. We'll have it without him, anyway. Well, it's our *duty* to, isn't it? How're we goin' to do acts of heroism same as Drake an' Dick Turpin an'—an' Guy Fawkes when we grow up if we don't get a bit of practice while we're young?"

"Who'll we have for members?" said Henry.

"Jus' us four," said William. "We'll call it the Adventure Society an' have jus' us four. We'll have meetin's an' passwords an'—an' do adventures."

"What sort of adventures?" said Henry.

William was silent for a few moments, then, "Well . . . findin' criminals an' nippin' their crimes in the bud, an' rescuin' people in deadly danger at peril of our lives," he said.

"How do we find 'em?" said Ginger.

"Go out an' look for 'em," said William. "It's Sat'day so we'll have all afternoon to do it. One adventure shouldn't take all that long. We'll meet in the old barn an' get it all fixed up. It's got to be a *secret* society with secret passwords an' things."

"What shall we have for a password?" said Henry.

"We'll have 'Down with Frenchie!' " said William.

"An' we'd better bring weapons 'cause we may be runnin' into deadly danger ourselves. You never know with adventures."

"Yes," agreed Henry. "We may find ourselves in some pretty tight corners."

They met in the old barn after lunch. They arrived separately, each uttering the words "Down with Frenchie!" as he entered the doorway.

William read the roll-call and each answered solemnly to his name as William called it out.

"Now we've got to take an oath," said William. "They always take oaths in secret societies. You can make up the oath, Henry. You're better at long words than us."

"All right," said Henry. He cleared his throat impressively then raised his right hand. "I swear never to betray the secrets of the Adventure Society an'—an' to carry out all its adventures"—he paused, at a loss momentarily for words then remembered the heading on one of his mother's tradesmen's bills and ended—"promptly and efficiently."

"That's jolly good," said William. "We needn't all say it 'case we don't remember it right. We'll jus' say, 'Hear, hear!' That's the same as sayin' it."

"Hear, hear!" said William, Henry and Ginger.

"Amen," said Douglas.

"We won't sign in blood," said William, " 'cause we haven't any paper an' the last time we did it, Ginger bled all over his new shirt an' Douglas wouldn't let us go deep enough to get any at all."

"It wasn't my fault," said Douglas. "I haven't got all that much blood in me, anyway. I did it in red ink in the end and it came to the same."

"It did *not*," said William. "Blood means you'll do something to the death, an' red ink jus' means you've pinched your father's bottle of red ink."

"It was my brother's," said Douglas. "They were usin' it for bloodstains in a play, so I didn't see why I shouldn't use it for real blood in real life."

"Oh shut up!" said William, "an' let's get on with fixin' up this society. We ought to have a secret sign."

"What sort of a secret sign?" said Ginger.

After a moment's consideration William raised both his arms above his head and slowly rotated his hands.

"Like this," he said. "Then when one of us makes it the others'll know he's a member of the secret Adventure Society."

"Well, we know that to start with, don't we?" said Douglas, who was still feeling a little sulky about the red ink, "an' it's not 'xactly a *secret* sign. I mean, people'd see us doin' it a mile off."

"Shut *up*!" said William again. "Anyway, we mus' have signs an' things for a secret society an' we mus' fix it up prop'ly to start with 'cause once it got goin' it might spread an' *spread*. It might come to be——"

"World-wide," suggested Henry.

"Yes, that," said William. "World-wide. So it's important to fix it up prop'ly to start with." He took a small red diary from his pocket. "I've brought this along. It's an old one of my mother's an' it's not got anythin' else in so we can use it to put things about the Society in, same as grown-ups do with their societies. Listen to what I've put down in it." He opened the book, turned over the pages and began to read in a loud throaty voice: "Adventure Society. By order. Members—William, Ginger, Henry, Douglas. Password, Down with Frenchie. One adventure to be done each week. As dangerous as possible. Deadly weapons may be used but axshul murder not allowed. Anyone betraying the secret of the Adventure Society wil be made to walk the plank in Jenks's pond. God Save the Queen!"

"That's jolly good," said Ginger.

"I bet you've spelt it all wrong," said Henry.

"Never mind how I've spelt it," said William, hastily closing the book and replacing it in his pocket. "It looks all right to me. I spell things the way they sound, which is a jolly sight more sens'ble than the way the diction'ry spells 'em. Gosh! If we all said things the way the diction'ry spells 'em we wouldn't know what we were talkin' about. Anyway, let's finish fixin' up this Adventure Society. We'll split into two lots an' go off diff'rent ways, 'cause it's no use too many people goin' after one adventure. They'd only get in a muddle. So I vote that Henry an' Douglas do the Hadley end an' me an' Ginger the Marleigh end. Then we'll meet here an' tell each other our adventures an' write 'em down in the book."

"We ought to elect a President, an' Secretary, an' Treasurer," said Henry.

"Well, there's no time for that," said William, "so I'll be all of 'em . . . Now let's start. We'll do the secret sign an' start straight away."

They went to the doorway and raised their arms solemnly in the secret sign.

"Down with Frenchie!" said William.

"Up with the Adventure Society!" said Ginger.

"For England and Saint George!" said Henry.

"I still think rats would be safer," said Douglas.

Henry and Douglas set off over the fields towards Hadley. William and Ginger went slowly to the stile that separated the field from the road.

"We'd better plan it out a bit first," said William. "We've got to think of the best place to find an adventure. We want a really good one."

"Not much chance of one round here," said Ginger, glancing round the familiar landscape.

"No, we've got to get right away from the places we *know*," said William. "Real adventures don't happen in the places people know. They happen in places people've never been in before. I mean, William the Conqueror had to come over here for the Battle of Hastings an' Christopher Columbus had to go to America to discover it."

"Yes, an' the North Pole," said Ginger vaguely.

"But there mus' be places not very far off that we've never been to," said William. "I mean, the world doesn't stop at Marleigh an' Steedham." He gave his ironic snort. "It'd be jolly funny if the world stopped at Marleigh an' Steedham."

"It'd make Geography a bit easier," said Ginger.

"Well, I vote we go to one of the farthest away places we know an' start off from there into some other place that's farther away still. We're bound to find an adventure in an unknown place."

"Well, which is the farthest place we know?" said Ginger.

"I think Steedham's the nearest place I've never been

much farther than," said William. "There's lots of roads goin' off from it. We might try that. We could go to Steedham by bus."

"It's eightpence each way," said Ginger.

"Well, it's bound to be a bit expensive," said William. "Adventures are . . . I bet that man Drake had to spend more than eightpence each way on his, and all that gunpowder Guy Fawkes bought mus' have cost a lot anyway. I've got that two an' six Robert gave me for keepin' out of the way when he had his girl friend to tea yesterday. An' I've got fourpence halfpenny left from my pocket money."

"An' I've got sixpence," said Ginger.

"Well, that's enough to go on with. It's enough to have a chocolate lolly on the way too to keep our strength up . . . Oh, an' there's weapons . . . I forgot to ask the others about weapons. I've brought my water pistol. I've filled it an' I'm keepin' it the right way up in my pocket. It could almost *blind* anyone if I got it right in his eyes. What have you got?"

Ginger drew an ancient penknife from his pocket.

"I've brought this. The knife's not much good but it's got a *fabulous* corkscrew. If I hit the right spot with it it'd give anyone a mortal injury."

"That's jolly good," said William. "We'll keep 'em hidden till we have to use 'em 'cause we don't want to rouse suspicion . . . Now come on. We'll call for that choc lolly then we'll catch the bus to Steedham."

The bus deposited them outside the post office at Steedham and they stood there for a moment or two, looking around. There was no one in sight. A large black cat sunned itself on a cottage window-sill and a baby slept peacefully in a pram outside the post office.

"Not much crime goin' on here," said Ginger in a tone of disapproval.

" 'Course not," said William. "Crimes don't go on with shops an' people all about. They go on in dark gloomy houses s'rounded by dark gloomy trees."

Again Ginger inspected the landscape.

"Well, there aren't any," he said.

" 'Course not," said William. "We've got to find 'em. We've got to go down lanes an' roads till we *do* find 'em . . . I've never been down that road that goes behind the church. Come on. Let's go down it."

They set off down the road behind the church. A few houses bordered the road, giving place gradually to woods and open fields.

"What sort of adventures are we lookin' for?" said Ginger.

"I told you," said William. "Rescuin' people in deadly peril or nippin' crimes in the bud."

"My mother was readin' about a crime in a book las' week," said Ginger. "About a man that kept his wife prisoner an' *tortured* her to make her sign a paper givin' him all her money."

"Yes, that's a good one," said William.

"It's s'posed to have really happened," said Ginger. "In France. A long time ago. But I don't see how it could have happened really."

"Why not?" said William.

"The p'lice'd find out an' stop 'em."

"They wouldn't know," said William. "It would all go on in this dark gloomy house s'rounded by dark gloomy trees that no one could see from the road."

"Yes, but she'd have friends an' sisters an' people who'd find out an' set her free."

"He might keep 'em *all* prisoners. He might have a sort of gang of—of thugs that he'd promised part of the money to an' they'd keep this woman an' all her friends prisoners an' *torture* them till she'd signed this paper."

"Yes, but the people who lived round . . . they'd find out."

"No, they wouldn't. They'd never see these women or these thugs. They'd jus' see the villain an' he'd seem an ordin'ry good man on the outside, same as—well, same as Frenchie. He might even have a job an' go off to it every mornin' jus' to put people off the scent, leavin' these thugs to keep these women prisoner an' torture them. He might even pretend to be a schoolmaster, same as Frenchie."

"Y-yes," said Ginger.

"I've been thinkin' . . ." said William after a pause. "It *did* seem a bit queer him gettin' so mad about our Adventure Society. It was sort of as if he'd got somethin' to hide . . . Come to think of it . . . we don't know much about him . . . jus' that he turns up to teach an' then goes away again. We don't really know what he really does."

"But he doesn't *seem* like a person to keep people prisoners an' torture them," said Ginger.

" 'Course he doesn't," said William. "I keep *tellin'* you. He's got to *act* like a good man so's he can get away with his crimes."

They walked on in silence for some minutes.

"But, you know, ole Frenchie couldn't *really* be a crim'nal," said Ginger.

"No, I s'pose he couldn't," said William, dismissing the idea with regret. "Never mind. Let's jus' go on lookin' for this adventure . . ."

"I s'pose any sort'd do," said Ginger.

"Yes . . ." said William. "You can't pick an' choose with adventures . . . If it was near the sea we might find someone cut off by the tide an' rescue him."

"Yes, but it isn't," said Ginger.

"Or we might find a lost an' starvin' animal an' restore it to its owners," said William. "It would be a bit savage with starvin' so it could count as an adventure . . . Or we could tackle a burglar gettin' out of a window with his loot."

"Sounds a bit dangerous," said Ginger.

"Well, it's got to be dangerous to be an adventure," said William. "A cat up a tree'd be better than nothin'. We could get it down at peril of our lives."

"The las' time we did that," said Ginger, "the cat got down all right by itself an' we got stuck in the tree an' had to be got down by ladders."

"Well, it wasn't our fault," said William. "The tree was the wrong shape."

They walked on down another road . . . down a lane . . . William's spirits began to flag.

"Gosh!" he said irritably, "you'd think *someone*'d get in a bit of danger *somewhere* wouldn't you? . . . Look! We'll jus' go to the end of this lane an' if we don't find anythin' we'll go back an' try again nex' week."

They walked on down the lane. Suddenly William stopped.

"Crumbs!" he said faintly. "Look!"

They gazed, spellbound and aghast. By the side of the lane an overgrown hedge almost concealed an overgrown garden. Beyond the hedge thickly planted trees almost concealed a grim-looking, barrack-like house.

"*Look!*" said William again. "A dark gloomy house s'rounded by dark gloomy trees."

"It mightn't be a crim'nal's house," said Ginger.

"I bet it is," said William. "Let's go nearer an' see . . ."

They crossed the road and stood in the gateway, looking up the tree-shadowed drive.

Then they gasped and clutched each other helplessly.

There was no mistaking the small red car that stood outside the front door.

They saw it every day in the school drive.

It was Mr. French's.

"Gosh!" breathed William.

The power of speech had almost deserted him.

"Yes, it's his all right," said Ginger. "He got that bump on his bumper goin' out of the school gate las' week . . . But—he might jus' be callin' there to see a friend."

William gave his ironic snort.

"It looks jolly funny to *me*," he said. "Come on. We've got to get to the bottom of it."

They crept up the drive under the shadow of the trees and round to the side of the house, where a large window gave a view of a bare unfurnished room with a screen set across the doorway. And again the boys gasped in horror and amazement. For, in front of the fireplace, stood Mr. French himself, his small face tensed and set. Around him stood five or six young men, looking equally grim and determined.

Suddenly from behind the screen came a woman, cowering in terror. One of the young men stepped forward and handed her a roll of paper. As she read it she burst into tears, thrusting out her arms in terror and despair.

"The paper!" whispered William. "The paper to sign away her money!"

The other young men darted behind the screen and dragged out more women weeping and cringing.

"The thugs!" said William.

The young men flung the women to the ground. One young man dragged a woman by the hair across the room. Another kicked a woman savagely as she lay sobbing . . . And Mr. French stood there, directing operations, obviously urging his thugs to further brutalities.

THE BOYS GASPED IN HORROR AND AMAZEMENT.

"Can't hear what any of them are saying, can you?" whispered Ginger.

"No," said William. "They mus' have had the windows made specially thick . . . Look!" His face froze in horror as one of the young men lifted a heavy stick and was obviously going to bring it down on the head of one of the women who lay outstretched on the floor. "Quick!" He drew Ginger away from the window into the shelter of one of the thick shrubs. "It's jus' what we said. He's got 'em all imprisoned an' him an' his thugs are torturin' them till they sign the paper. It's a crime all right an' we've got to nip it in the bud."

"Let's fetch the p'lice," said Ginger.

**AROUND MR. FRENCH STOOD FIVE OR SIX YOUNG MEN,
LOOKING EQUALLY GRIM AND DETERMINED.**

"Gosh, no!" said William. "It'd take too long. We've got to rescue them now, quick!"

"How?" said Ginger, sending a wistful glance at the open road.

"*Tell* you what!" said William. "That was a pretty big screen in front of the door. We'll get behind it—I bet there's some chairs there we can stand on an' fix Mr. French. He's the real crim'nal. The thugs are jus' in his pay, so he's the one we've got to nip in the bud . . . Listen! I'll shoot my water pistol into his eyes—I've kept it the right way up an' it ought to work—an' you throw your corkscrew at him. Try'n' get the top of his head 'cause that's where people's brains are. That ought to knock him out an' the thugs won't know what to do without him to tell them, an' the victims can escape before he comes to."

"Yes, but——" began Ginger.

"Oh, come on!" said William impatiently.

He made his way round the house to the front door, followed by Ginger. He tried the handle. It opened. He stepped into a large old-fashioned hall. He tiptoed to the nearest door and opened it cautiously. It was the room they had seen through the window. The large screen hid most of the interior of the room, but there were two chairs against the wall inside the door. Soundlessly William and Ginger moved them till they were just behind the screen. They climbed on to them . . .

"Got your corkscrew ready?" whispered William. "Now! One, two three, *go!*"

But William had leant unguardedly against the screen in order to discharge his water pistol, and suddenly the whole thing collapsed. It was a heavy screen and it fell heavily upon the occupants of the room. Screams, groans, shouts of rage rose from beneath it. Obeying the simple instinct of self-preservation, William and Ginger fled from the room, down a passage, out of a back door, across a stretch of ground and into a building that was evidently a sort of outhouse.

"I thought we'd better get out at the back," panted William. "They'd have seen us through the window if we'd gone out by the front . . . Gosh! If those thugs get hold of us . . . !" He looked around. There was a loft above them with an open trapdoor and a ladder fixed in place. There came the sound of footsteps and voices, drawing nearer . . .

"The thugs!" panted William. "Come on quick! Up the ladder!"

Hastily they climbed the ladder, reaching a loft that was empty except for a pile of sacks in one corner and rows of apples spread out on the floor.

"They'll find us here," said Ginger.

"No, they won't," said William. "They won't think of lookin' here."

He dropped the ladder on to the ground and lowered the trapdoor, leaving an opening of a few inches.

Almost immediately two men entered the outhouse and looked about them.

"Milly said that she distinctly saw two boys taking to their heels when the screen fell . . . Well, they aren't here, anyway."

"There's some sort of loft up there."

"But the ladder's not in place. They'd never have got up there."

"Actually, you know, I'm rather vague as to what it's all about. Milly asked me to help with the costumes and I came along to watch a rehearsal and get the hang of the thing, but I still don't quite know what the thing is."

"Well, nearly all these little country villages have their own little amateur dramatic societies, you know, and they have a joint Drama Festival every year with a sort of competition. And this year the subject of the competition was some historical event to be performed in mime. Milly's gang decided to do the Dissolution of the Monasteries . . . You know . . . brutal soldiery evicting helpless nuns. Milly was to be the abbess. She put up a good act when they showed her the King's decree dissolving her convent, didn't she? It was a bit hard on them having to do it in mime, of course. A few good screams would have put some body into it. I think the screen fell down of its own accord, but Milly insists that she saw two boys . . ."

"How did Mr. French come into it?"

The other laughed.

"Oh, old French has cherished a hopeless passion for Milly for years, and I think that Milly's cherished one for him, but they're both so shy that nothing's ever come of it. Anyway, when she asked him to take on the job of producer he jumped at it, of course. Actually he's an excellent producer, though he gets furious when they don't do exactly what he tells them even before he's told them. I wish he and Milly would get spliced. They're about the same age and it would get her out of this gloomy old house. They're both decent types . . . Well, I suppose we may consider the rehearsal at an end now, so I'll give up the chase of the mythical boys and be making tracks for home."

The voices died away in the distance.

"Let's have a shot at getting down now," said William. "I bet I can jump."

But other voices were approaching and, looking down, William saw Mr. French entering the building with the pleasant-faced, middle-aged woman who had taken the part of the abbess.

"I've been trying to ask you for years," said Mr. French.

"But why didn't you?" said Milly. "I've been hoping you would for years."

"I couldn't pluck up courage," said Mr. French, "but when I saw the screen fall on you and thought for a dreadful second that you were dead, I couldn't keep it in any longer. It just came out."

"I've often wondered how to bring you to the point," said Milly. "Somehow I never thought of getting someone to knock a screen down on to me."

Mr. French gave his rusty laugh.

"Well, you've made me very happy, my dear," he said.

WILLIAM SAW MR. FRENCH ENTERING THE BUILDING WITH THE PLEASANT-FACED, MIDDLE-AGED WOMAN.

"And you've made me," said Milly simply.

"But I can see no traces of the mysterious boys," said Mr. French. "I think, my dear, that you imagined them."

"I may have done," said Milly. "I'm in no condition to know what's real and what isn't."

"Well, you're real and I'm real and that's all that matters," said Mr. French.

Their voices died away into the distance.

"Let's get out of here," said William tersely. "I've had jus' about enough of it."

They found a small window and a fig tree that grew conveniently up the wall outside it and made their way quickly out at the back—through the back garden and into a lane that led to the main road. There they stopped to draw breath.

"I've had enough of Frenchie to last me the rest of my life," said William bitterly. "First he pretends to be an ordin'ry person an' turns out to be a crim'nal an' then he pretends to be a crim'nal an' turns out to be an ordin'ry person. I'm just' about sick of crim'nals *an*' ordin'ry persons."

"It's not his fault," said Ginger. "He can't help not bein' a crim'nal . . . An' we ought to think kindly of him now he's goin' to be married."

"Yes, an' we'll have to help pay for his weddin' present an' we've spent all our money on him already. We've only got a halfpenny left. It ought to be him givin' us a wedding present not us givin' him."

"Yes, but it's him that's goin' to be married," Ginger pointed out.

"Yes, but it's us that's wasted all that money on bus fares over that adventure that he went an' messed up. Come to think of it, he owes us for the choc lollies, too, 'cause we only bought them to give us strength for his rotten ole adventure."

"We'd better be gettin' back home," said Ginger nervously. "They might be sendin' out more people to look for us."

"I'm goin' to put down our expenses in our Adventure Society book first," said William, "an' find out how much he owes us." He put his hand into his pocket and a blank look came over his face. "Gosh! I haven't got it. I had it when we started out. It mus' have fallen out of my pocket in that room when the screen fell down. I'm goin' back to get it."

"You *can't*, William," protested Ginger. "Not into the jaws of danger like that!"

"Well, it might turn out to be a bit of an adventure, after all," said William, his spirits rising. "I'm goin' back to get it anyway. You'd better not come. It's easier for one person to get out of the jaws of danger than two. You can sit on that stile an' wait for me. If I'm not back in an hour you'd better get in touch with Scotland Yard. They made out it was only play-actin' but they looked a nasty lot of people. I bet they'd stick at nothin'."

He set off jauntily down the road. Ginger took his seat on the lowest rung of the stile, resting his chin on his hands. His face wore a woebegone expression. He was wondering how one got in touch with Scotland Yard and how he could manage it without William to help him. It seemed to him that more than an hour had passed (though really it was only ten minutes) before William appeared, walking round the bend of the road.

"I've got it," he said. "They were all lookin' for us in the wood at the bottom of the garden an' there was no one in that room at all. It was lyin' on the floor jus' where the screen fell down."

"Well, come on! Let's get back to the old barn quick before anythin' else happens," said Ginger.

"Yes, I 'spect Henry an' Douglas have got back there now," said William.

Henry and Douglas were standing in the doorway of the old barn waiting for them. They had only been able to achieve one adventure—that of finding a lost dog and restoring it to its owner but, as it turned out that the dog was not lost and was making its way home by a familiar route, the adventure had fallen a little flat.

William gave a highly coloured account of his and Ginger's adventure.

"Soon as they found we were on their tracks they tried to pretend it was all play-actin' but—huh!—they didn't take *me* in! An' they tried to pinch our Adventure Society book but they didn't get away with *that* either. Let's write down about 'em now."

He took the red pocket diary from his pocket and opened it, then gasped in dismay.

"Gosh! It's not my book." He turned over the pages. "It's ole Frenchie's. It's got his name an' address in it an' names of meetin's he's goin' to an' trains he's goin' by an' names of books he's goin' to get from the library an' stuff like that. Gosh! It's exactly like mine. He mus' have dropped it like me when the screen came down."

"What'll we do with it?" said Ginger.

"Dunno," said William. He was still turning over the pages. "It's no use to us. It doesn't say anythin' about his life of crime." He closed the book. "Tell you what! We'll post it to him. It's got his name and address in so the postman ought to know where to take it. Anyway, if it gets to him it gets to him an' if it doesn't it doesn't."

The others agreed. They walked down the field to the road. And here they stopped suddenly. For Mr. French was coming down the road, walking briskly, humming to himself.

"Oh, Brown!" he said. "The very boy I wanted to see." He took a small red pocket diary from his pocket. "This, I believe, is your property."

William's face was blank and expressionless.

"Thanks," he said. He took the other diary from his pocket and handed it to Mr. French. " 'N' this looks like yours. Seems to've got into my pocket somehow."

Mr. French made a grating sound that might have been a cough or a chuckle.

"Exactly, exactly! Well, I won't inquire into your dubious activities this afternoon too closely, because, as it happens"—his features creased into a tight little smile—"they turned out very well for me personally. Very well indeed. And, to mark the happy occasion, I'll reverse the decision I made about your Adventure Society. I will give you permission to have it. I will even offer myself as a patron. I may live to regret it, but I am in the mood to make rash decisions just now. You see before you a lucky and a very happy man."

He strode off down the road, humming again to himself. They watched him in gloomy silence till he had disappeared, then returned slowly to the old barn. "Crumbs!" said William disgustedly. "*Him* a patron! An' *lettin'* us have it! When he's *ruined* the whole thing from beginnin' to end. Well, I wouldn't have an Adventure Society now if he *paid* me for it!"

An air of depression had fallen over the group.

"All that trouble for nothin'!" said Ginger.

" 'The best laid plans of mice an' men——' " said Henry.

William brightened. His listlessness fell from him.

"Yes, that's an idea," he said. "Let's go to the old stables near Frankie's house an' have a look at them. We'll call at our homes for a bit of food an' try catchin' an' tamin' them. I bet we could *train* 'em all right too. We could have a *circus* of them. Jumpin' through hoops. Ridin' on each other's backs. Turnin' somersaults . . . They're jolly intelligent. I bet they'd *like* it!"

He was silent for a moment, seeing himself in the centre of a 'ring', whip in hand, uttering short sharp orders to the rats that circled round him, jumping through hoops, riding on each other's backs, turning somersaults, walking tightropes, driving miniature motor-cars, beating miniature drums, marching in formation, dancing . . . His Rat

Circus was famous throughout the world. It appeared on television. It visited the capitals of every civilised country. People queued up for miles, paid fantastic sums to see it.

"Come on!" he said eagerly. "Let's get started on it."

"I wonder if they like liqu'rice allsorts," said Ginger. "I've got some at home."

"There's a poem about 'em likin' music," said Henry. "I could call at home for my mouth organ."

"Oh come *on!*" said William.

They ran down the field to the stile. Douglas was the last, falling over the stile into the road in his haste.

"I said rats all along," he panted as he scrambled to his feet.

Chapter 6

William's Long and Tiring Day

William entered by the front door, gave his feet a perfunc-
tory scrape on the mat, scattering clods of mud in all
directions, picked up several of the largest and slipped
them into his pocket in an attempt to avert his parents'
wrath, stood in front of the mirror for a few moments
practising his Face (he'd thought of a forward and sideways thrust that improved it considerably) then took his
father's walking-stick from the hatstand and, using it as
a jumping pole, tried to leap the gulf that separated the
end of the hatstand from the bottom step of the staircase.
He missed the bottom step and fell with a clatter on to
the floor.

"What on *earth* are you doing, William?" called his
mother from the sitting-room.

"Nothin'," said William, picking himself up.

"Then stop doing it at once," called his father severely.

"And go and wash your face and brush your hair," said
his mother. "I'm sure they need it."

"A' right," said William.

He went up the first few steps then stopped. Through

"HE CARRIED ON LIKE SOMEONE OUT OF A MADHOUSE,"
ROBERT WAS SAYING.

the half-open door he could see his father and mother
sitting on either side of the fireplace and his elder brother
Robert standing between them. They were evidently
taking up a conversation that had been interrupted by
the sounds of his home-coming. Robert's voice was high-
pitched and indignant. William stayed to listen.

"He carried on like someone out of a madhouse,"
Robert was saying. "Called me every name he could lay
his hands on."

"Where exactly did it happen?" said Mr. Brown.

"At the cross-roads," said Robert.

"And what exactly did happen?" said Mrs. Brown.

"Well, I was coming into the cross-roads very carefully. I certainly wasn't speeding when his car shot into the cross-roads out of Marleigh Road, doing seventy at least and heading straight into me."

"What was the damage?" said Mr. Brown.

"There wasn't any damage," said Robert. "He rammed on his brakes and skidded round in circles, but there wasn't even a scratch, and it was all his fault, anyway. He's a public menace . . . He got out of his car, cursed me up hill and down dale and said he was going to report me to the police for dangerous driving."

"Gosh!" said William, appearing suddenly in the doorway. "It ought to be you reportin' him. It——"

"Get out!" said Robert.

"Who did you say the man was?" said Mr. Brown.

"Chap called Newgate," said Robert. "I've met him at the tennis club but I hardly know him . . . You should have seen him—purple in the face and cursing like a trooper. Shook his fist at me and nearly punched me on the nose."

"You ought to have clobbered him," said William. "You——"

"Get *out*!" said Robert savagely.

William got out.

"And do wash your face and brush your hair, dear," called Mrs. Brown.

But William thought that his face and hair could wait. He went quietly out of the front door and made his way to Ginger's house.

He found Ginger in the garden busy with his fish pond. Ginger's mother had given him a small plot of ground at the end of the lawn for his own particular use and an aunt had given him a selection of suitable garden plants. Ginger, whose tastes did not run to the horticultural, had exchanged the plants for a goldfish in a bowl that Victor Jameson had won at a fête and was engaged in turning his garden into a fish pond for the goldfish. He had dug out the soil to what he considered the right depth and, with the aid of a trowel, was lining the hole with a splodgy mess of watery cement. He had been working on it for the last hour and now presented a spectral appearance beneath a dusting of white powder. The goldfish, named Lion Heart by Victor, watched anxiously from its bowl at the edge of the lawn.

"It doesn't seem to *stick* properly," said Ginger. "It just soaks down into the soil. I think I've put too much water in, I'll put some more cement in."

He took up a bag and tipped some more cement into the hole, enveloping himself and William in a white cloud.

"Never mind that," said William impatiently, moving the white cloud away with his hand. "We've got more important things to think of than that now."

"What?" said Ginger, laying aside his trowel and wiping his hands down his trousers.

"Robert," said William. "He's in danger."

"What sort of danger?" said Ginger.

"Deadly danger," said William. "He's goin' to be handed over to the p'lice."

"Gosh!" said Ginger. "What's he done? He's not murdered anyone, has he?"

"No, no," said William, "But it's almost as bad. He'll be tried by a judge in a court of law an' he might be sent to prison for *years*. This man that's a public menace'll stop at nothin'."

"But what happened?" said Ginger.

"Well, this man that's a public menace came chargin' at Robert in his car. I bet he was tryin' to—to run him down. I bet he was tryin' to sort of put him out of the way."

"Why was he?" said Ginger.

"We don't know yet," said William mysteriously. "In books it's always 'cause the person they try to run down has found some guilty secret about the villain, so the villain's got to put him out of the way before he tells anyone."

"What sort of a guilty secret was it?" said Ginger, wiping cement from his lips with the back of his hand.

"We don't know," said William. "Axshully, it might not have been one 'cause Robert isn't the sort of person to find out guilty secrets. I bet he wouldn't know they were guilty ones even if he did find them out . . . but prob'ly this public menace *thought* he'd found one out so he tried to run him down to get rid of him. But Robert was too quick for him an' managed to dodge him. He only jus' escaped with his life."

"Gosh!" said Ginger spitting out a mouthful of cement. "It's got a funny sort of taste . . . What happened then?"

"Well, that's the worst part of it, what happened then," said William. "You see, he was *mad* 'cause he'd not been able to get rid of Robert by runnin' him down, so he thought he'd get him put away by bringin' a false accusation against him. He thought that if he could get him imprisoned for life for dangerous driving his guilty secret would be safe."

"I don't think you can get imprisoned for life for dangerous driving," said Ginger.

"I bet this man could fix it," said William. "I told you he'd stop at nothin' . . . Anyway, even if he didn't get him imprisoned for life he'd prob'ly get him disqualified from drivin' for life an' then he'd have to go about on foot an' it'd give this villain another chance of runnin' him down."

"Sounds pretty bad," said Ginger, "but what can we do?"

"We've got to get him out of the clutches of this villain," William said.

"How?" said Ginger, taking up the trowel again and moving it slowly through the splodgy mess.

"Well, we can't make any def'nite plans till we know more about him," said William. "We know his name—his name's Newgate—but I don't know where he lives. You see . . ."

The voice of Ginger's mother cut William's sentence short.

"Bedtime!" she called from an upstairs window. "Off you go, William!"

"We'll meet tomorrow," said William hastily. "We'll try'n' find out where he lives an' fix up a plan . . . You find out where he lives an' I'll fix up a plan."

William's mother was in the hall when he reached home. Her voice rose in horror when she saw him.

"William, what on *earth's* happened to your clothes?"

William glanced down at his clothes.

"Jus'—jus' normal wear an' tear, I 'spect," he said, remembering a phrase he had heard used in connection with an insurance claim.

"William, it *couldn't* be."

William appeared to consider deeply.

"Well," he said, "it might—it jus' might be a bit of cement."

William and Ginger met at the corner of the road that led to Ginger's house.

"Was your mother mad with you?" said William.

"Yes," said Ginger. "Was yours?"

"Yes," said William, "but never mind that now . . . It's Robert we've got to think of now. Have you found out where this Newgate man lives?"

"Yes," said Ginger. "He lives at that house called 'Homefield', jus' near the new estate . . . Have you thought of a plan?"

William was silent for a few moments. Last night he had been convinced that Robert was the victim of a deep and nefarious plot . . . but in the cold light of morning he was less sure.

"Well, I think prob'ly it was jus' what he said . . . jus' this public menace man drivin' dangerously an' tryin' to put it on Robert."

"Then you don't think Robert had found out a guilty secret?" said Ginger, disappointed.

"No, no, but it's almost as bad," said William. "I mean, think of poor old Robert tried in a court of law an' put in prison, an' it's jolly serious. It'll give him what's called a crim'nal record an' it'll go against him all his life. He'll never be able to get a decent job 'cause of this crim'nal record. Whenever he tries to get one they'll ask him if he's got a crim'nal record an' he'll have to say he has an' they'll turn him down."

"Have you thought of a plan, then?" said Ginger.

"Yes, I've thought of a plan all right," said William. "You see, I don't think this man's a *real* villain, same as I thought he was at first, but that won't make it any better for Robert's crim'nal record. I think he's jus' an ordin'ry, inyuman, hard-hearted man an' we've got to do something to sort of melt his heart."

"What?" said Ginger.

"Well, I thought we'd go to this house where he lives an' say we'll do odd jobs for him an' then we'll do every-thing we *can* to help him an' melt his heart an' when we've got it melted we'll say we don't want money, we jus' want him not to report Robert to the p'lice for dangerous drivin'.."

"Y-yes," said Ginger." It *sounds* all right . . ."

"It *is* all right," said William. "It's a jolly good plan an' Robert'll be jolly grateful." The mental picture of a grateful Robert was somehow difficult to conjure up, but he continued, "He's *sure* to be grateful. Stands to reason he will. Anyone'd be grateful to be saved from a crim'nal record. Well, its news to *me* if they wouldn't."

"When do we start?" said Ginger.

"Now," said William.

'Homefield' was a small, squat house with small squat windows and a skimpy roof that looked like an ill-fitting cap. The place had a surly, unwelcoming air and seemed to scowl suspiciously at the two boys as they made their way up the short drive. They took up their positions side by side on the top step, then William raised the knocker and performed the loud and lengthy tattoo with which he was wont to announce his arrival at the homes of his acquaintances. A woman with a large flabby face and untidy grey hair opened the door. She wore a grimy overall, secured in front by a massive safety-pin, and carried a dishcloth in one hand.

" 'Ere! What's the idea?" she said. "Knockin' the place down!"

William bared his teeth in what was meant to be an ingratiating smile.

" 'Scuse me," he said. "Does Mr. Newgate live here? I mean, if it's not troublin' you too much . . ."

"It's troublin' me all right," said the woman, "knockin' the place down! What'd you want with 'im?"

"We've come to do odd jobs," said William, sustaining the ingratiating smile with difficulty.

"For nothin'," said Ginger.

"Well, you've started on 'em all right," said the woman, "knockin' the place down."

"Who is it, Mrs. Hemlock?" snapped an irritable voice behind her.

"Two boys," said the woman, "wantin' odd jobs, knockin' the place down."

The man who came to the door was short and harassed-looking, with hair neatly parted in the middle and a mouth that seemed to be pursed in permanent disapproval. He peered shortsightedly at William and Ginger.

"Well, what is it?" he said.

"Ooligans," said the woman.

"We're *not* hooligans," said William indignantly. "We've come to do odd jobs, to *help*."

"For nothin'," said Ginger.

"Go on!" said the woman.

" 'Cause of this public menace," said Ginger.

"Shut up!" said William.

The man looked at them more closely. William, unable to sustain the ingratiating smile, had assumed the ferocious scowl that was part of his defensive armour against life in general. The scowl seemed to reassure Mr. Newgate. It seemed to express reliability, integrity and earnestness of purpose.

"Well, well," he said, "it so happens that there is something I want done and I've no time to attend to it myself. I see no reason why you shouldn't do it. It's a perfectly simple job. Come this way."

He led them down the passage to a small conservatory. A table stood in the middle and plants were ranged on stages round the sides. he took a box from one of the stages and poured a cascade of nails of every shape and size on to the table.

"I want these sorting out into sizes," he said. "I've been meaning to do it for months but haven't been able to get down to it."

"He's a jolly good driver really, you know," said William.

"I'll find you some tins to put them in," said Mr. Newgate.

"He's sometimes driven for *months* without an accident," said Ginger.

"This'll do for the largest," said Mr. Newgate, bringing a tin from beneath the stages.

"He passed his test almost at once," said William, adding, "Well, nearly almost."

"This will do for the medium-sized ones," said Mr. Newgate.

"It mus' have been a bit your fault," said Ginger.

"I can't find anything for the smallest ones," said Mr. Newgate. "Oh, this would do."

"A crim'nal record would ruin his whole life," said William.

But it was clear that Mr. Newgate, intent on finding boxes and tins to fit the nails, was not listening to them.

"Now stop chattering, boys," he said at last, "and get down to work as quickly as you can. I have to go into Hadley to the bank and the library and I shall expect to find them all sorted out neatly into sizes when I come back . . . And, Mrs. Hemlock"—Mrs. Hemlock had appeared in the doorway and was watching the scene with an expression of sardonic amusement—"I want you to do the paintwork in the sitting-room while I'm away and put the stew on the gas cooker and cut the onions up into it. And straighten the pictures in my study. You've left them all crooked again. And dust the top of the bookcase. It's *thick* with dust. You can't have touched it for weeks. I don't know what you *do* with your time . . . Where are my library books? Where's my hat? Where are my gloves? Keep your eye on those boys . . . and get out of my way."

There came the sound of the slamming of the front door and Mr. Newgate hurried past the window, muttering to himself.

William and Ginger stood gazing gloomily at the nails.

"That's goin' to take a bit of time," said Ginger, "an' he didn't listen to a word we said."

"Yes, it's a *labour* all right," said William. "Same as that man Hercules in the fairy tale."

"It wasn't a fairy tale," said Ginger. "It was in hist'ry. It . . ."

Mrs. Hemlock appeared suddenly in the doorway. She was ramming a cloth cap over her head and shrugging herself into an ancient raincoat. Her face was set in lines of fury.

"Well, I've 'ad enough of 'im," she said. " 'Im an' is sauce! 'Oo does 'e think 'e is? King of the Cannibal Isles? I've 'ad enough of bein' treated like an 'eathen slave. It's a long worm that 'as no turnin', but this worm's been drove up the wall once too often an' it's turnin' good an' proper, 'ere an' now. 'E can straighten 'is *own* pictures an' dust 'is *own* bookcase an' do 'is *own* paintwork an' put onions in 'is *own* stew . . . Doesn't know what I do with me time, doesn't 'e? Well, you can *tell* 'im what I'm doin' with me time. I'm packin' up on 'im with me time. I'm gettin' shut of 'im fer good an' all with me time an' you can tell 'im *that* with me compliments. Good-*bye*."

She gave a final twist to the raincoat, a final tug at the cap and flounced out of the room. Again the slamming of the front door echoed through the house.

William and Ginger looked at each other.

"Well," said Ginger at last, "what do we do now?"

"*Tell* you what!" said William after a moment's pause. "We'll do the things she was s'posed to be doin'. That ought to put him in a good temper an' melt his heart."

"There's the nails . . ." said Ginger.

William threw a distasteful glance at the nails.

"Let's do the other things first," he said, "paintwork an' onions an' things. They're a bit more intr'estin' than nails. We'll leave the nails to the last."

"All right," said Ginger. "What'll we start with?"

"Paintwork," said William.

They went into the sitting-room and looked around.

"I 'spect it's the wooden parts he wants paintin'," said William.

"Where's the paint?" said Ginger.

"It'll be somewhere about," said William. "Let's have a look . . ."

Ginger opened the cupboard under the stairs and burrowed among a heap of odds and ends.

"Yes, here it is!" he said at last, "but it's green paint an' the wood in the sittin'-room's painted white."

"I spect he wants a change," said William. "Is there a brush, too?"

"Yes, here's a brush."

"All right. You start on the paintin' an' I'll start on the stew. We'll do it quick so's we'll have it all done by the time he comes back an' put him in a good temper straight away."

Ginger took up paint tin and brush and went into the sitting-room. William went into the kitchen. They continued their conversation through the open doors.

"I'm startin' on the skirtin' board next to the floor," said Ginger. "It's good paint but it doesn't stick on very well. It runs down on to the floor."

"Stir it up a bit," said William.

"A'right . . . How're you gettin' on?"

"Not bad. I've found the stew in a saucepan an' put it on a gas ring. It should be all right."

"I think I'll try paintin' the window-sills. I think it'll

stay on better on the window-sills . . . Remember he said
onions in the stew."

"Yes, I'm lookin' for 'em."

"It does stay on better on the window-sills. They sort
of hold it up . . . Have you found the onions?"

"No . . . Oh, yes. Here they are. In a basket on the
step outside the kitchen door. Funny place to keep them."

"You've got to peel them an' cut them up, you know."

"Yes, I'm doin' that."

"It's not stickin' on the window-sills very well now. It's
started droppin' off on to the floor."

"I 'spect you're puttin' on too much."

"P'raps . . . How're you gettin' on?"

"All right. The peel comes off quite easy."

"They make you cry, don't they?"

"These don't. I 'spect they're a specially good sort."

They worked in silence for some time.

"I've nearly finished this tin of paint," said Ginger.

"I've got the stew boilin'," said William. "I've found a
spoon an' I'm stirrin' it to keep it goin'."

There came the sound of the opening and shutting of
the front door.

"He's back," whispered William.

Quick footsteps crossed the hall . . . then Mr. Newgate
entered the kitchen.

"Where's Mrs. Hemlock?" he said.

"She's gone," said William. "She told us to tell you
she was goin' for good an' all."

"Oh, she does that regularly once a fortnight," said Mr.
Newgate. "She'll be back tomorrow. Probably annoyed
because I told her to dust the bookcase and wash down
the paintwork."

"W-wash down?" said William. "D-did you mean jus'
wash down?"

"Of course . . . What are you doing here anyway?

Have you finished sorting out the nails?" He opened the door that led out into the small back garden and his voice rose to a high note of exasperation. "What on earth has the woman done with my tulip bulbs? I left them here on the step ready for planting this afternoon. There's a warning of frost and I want to get them in as soon as I can . . . Where on earth can she have put them?"

William gazed at him blankly.

"Were they tulip bulbs?" he stammered.

"Were *what* tulip bulbs? What are you talking about?"

"I thought they were onions," said William desperately. "I've put them in the stew."

"You've put them in the stew! My tulip bulbs! My Darwin Specials?"

Mr. Newgate's scream of rage was cut short by the sight of Ginger, who appeared in the doorway, holding a dripping paint brush. Mr. Newgate choked convulsively for a few moments then, gibbering with rage, flung himself furiously in Ginger's direction.

Obeying the simple instinct of self preservation, William and Ginger dropped spoon and paint brush and fled—out of the front door, down the drive and into the road. The high-pitched voice—raised to a yet higher pitch as Mr. Newgate discovered the condition of his sitting-room—followed them.

"I'll tell your parents . . . I'll see that you're punished. I'll . . . I'll . . . I'll . . ."

The two paused for breath as they neared Ginger's house.

"We didn't melt his heart," said Ginger.

"No," agreed William, "but one good thing! He doesn't know who we are."

"He'll find out," said Ginger. "They always do. Shouldn't be surprised if he's not found out already . . . I don't think I want to go home jus' yet, do you?"

HE FLUNG HIMSELF FURIOUSLY IN GINGER'S DIRECTION.

"No," said William. "Let's have a bit of a walk round."

They had a bit of a walk round, discussing Ginger's fish-pond in a desultory, half-hearted fashion.

"I don't think that cement's goin' to work," said William. "I think it would be better to jus' dig a hole an' put a sort of tin in it."

"There's an old petrol tin in our garage," said Ginger.

"Don't be daft," said William. "We couldn't *see* him in a petrol tin. It's got to be one with a wide open top that'll *look* like a pond."

"I s'pose so," said Ginger.

They walked on in silence for some minutes.

"P'raps we'd better go home an' see what's happenin'," said William at last.

States of uncertainty never appealed to William. He was a boy whose temperament demanded action, however unpleasant.

"A' right," agreed Ginger. "A good thing my mother's out, I can get a bit of paint off before she comes back."

Slowly, apprehensively, William entered the sitting-room. His mother sat on one side of the fireplace knitting. His father sat on the other, reading a newspaper. They greeted him casually. He drew a sigh of relief. Evidently no complaint had yet reached them. Robert entered just as the telephone bell rang. Mrs. Brown went to answer it. She returned looking slightly bewildered.

"It's Mr. Newgate," she said.

"It'll be for you, Robert," said Mr. Brown. "About that motor-cycle business. I expect he's laid his hands on some fresh names to call you."

"It can't be that," said Robert. "I ran into him near the station just now and he apologised for losing his temper. He said it was just as much his fault as mine and he wouldn't dream of reporting me to the police."

"And he didn't seem to want to speak to Robert," said Mrs. Brown. "He specially asked if Mr. Brown Senior was at home and said he was coming round immediately to speak to him on a very important matter."

"What on earth can he want with me?" said Mr. Brown.

"It may not be my Newgate at all," said Robert. "There's another Newgate who lives at 'Homefield' on the way to Marleigh. I think they're distantly related, but they don't see much of each other. I believe the Homefield one's a crusty old devil."

"He sounded querulous," said Mrs. Brown. "Where are you going, dear?"

"Jus' out," said William.

He found Ginger hovering outside the gate.

"Anythin' happened?" said Ginger.

"He's found out who we are," said William.

"I knew he would," said Ginger.

"An' he's the wrong man," said William. "He's not the public menace an' anyway the public menace has stopped bein' one."

"Gosh!" said Ginger.

"An' he's jus' rung up my father to say he's comin' over to see him at once."

"*Gosh!*" said Ginger again. "What'll we do, then?"

"Let's go for another walk around," said William. "If they get a bit anxious an' wonder if somethin's happened to us it might sort of soften them."

"It never does," said Ginger gloomily. "It makes them madder than ever; I've tried it."

"Well, we'll go for a walk round, anyway," said William. "It puts things off for a bit anyway."

"A' right," agreed Ginger.

They walked on down the road . . . then suddenly they

stopped. Dusk was falling and a slight mist hung over the landscape, but there was no mistaking the taut little figure that was making its way towards them. Even the sound of the angry mutterings was by now familiar.

"It's him," whispered William. "Quick! Let's hide."

He was drawing Ginger towards the dry ditch that ran by the side of the road when suddenly the little figure flung out its arms and fell headlong. It was clear that Mr. Newgate had slipped on a muddy patch of road. Instinctively William and Ginger ran to help him, but he had scrambled to his feet when they reached him.

"My spectacles!" he gasped. "I was wearing them. Where are they?"

Ginger picked up his spectacles and handed them to him.

"Cracked!" said Mr. Newgate. "Dear! Dear! Dear! Cracked! Oh, well, I can just see my way without them and I have a spare pair at home." He clapped his hand to his pocket and his voice rose shrilly. "My cigarette-case! I had it in my pocket. It's gone. What's happened to it? Where is it? Where is it?"

William and Ginger searched the roadside. Suddenly Ginger caught the gleam of silver at the bottom of the dry ditch. He plunged down, retrieved the case and handed it to Mr. Newgate.

"Oh, thank you, thank you," said Mr. Newgate. "I wouldn't have lost it for anything in the world . . . I feel a little shaky. I think I'll sit down for a moment."

They were near the bus stop and the seat where would-be passengers whiled away the time between the erratic and unpredictable comings and goings of the Hadley bus.

They sat down . . . Mr. Newgate gazed fondly at his cigarette-case.

"I wouldn't have lost it for anything," he said again. "My father gave it to me on my twenty-first birthday

**GINGER RETRIEVED THE CASE, AND HANDED IT TO
MR. NEWGATE**

fifty years ago . . . Nice old chap, he was. Kind, good-
tempered, easy going. I'm the same, you know. Nothing
ever puts me out."

They threw him startled glances, but it was clear that
he believed what he was saying.

"Well, well, I'm lucky to have run into a couple of
kind, good, helpful little boys like you—and just when I
was on my way to complain of a couple of destructive
young hooligans"—his voice suddenly quivered with
anger—"who have almost wrecked my home."

"They—they—they didn't mean to," said William in a
hoarse, unnatural voice.

"Why?" said Mr. Newgate. "Do you know about it?"

"Well, we—we jus' heard about it," said William.

"Jus' in a sort of way," said Ginger, introducing a slight falsetto note into his voice.

"Do you know the boys?" said Mr. Newgate.

"Well, in a sort of way . . ." said William.

"We've *heard* of them," said Ginger.

"We know 'em by sight," said William.

"They're not friends of yours, I hope?"

"Oh, no," said William, "but"—with a burst of inspiration—"we go to the same school."

"I see. So, of course, you have to keep on friendly terms with them."

"Yes," said Ginger, letting his falsetto get a little out of hand, "yes, we've got to keep on friendly terms with them."

"An'—an'," said William, with another burst of inspiration, "our parents know their parents."

"I see," said Mr. Newgate again. "So you don't want their parents to be worried."

"Yes, that's it," said William, his hoarseness deepening almost to a growl, "we don't want their parents to be worried."

"Well, I must say the feeling does you credit," said Mr. Newgate. "Very great credit. But I shouldn't get too friendly with them. They're a most objectionable type— not at all suitable friends for you. Evil communications corrupt good manners, you know."

"Yes," said William. "I'm always sayin' that to them. I keep goin' on at 'em about it."

"On the other hand, of course, you might try to use your influence on them for good."

"Yes," said William. "We do that, all right. We're always usin' it on 'em."

"Perhaps after all," said Mr. Newgate slowly and thoughtfully, "a few well chosen words from you might do them more good than a punishment."

"That's what we've been thinkin'," said William earnestly.

"We've got a lot of words we could choose for 'em," said Ginger.

"I must say," said Mr. Newgate, "you're a couple of kind-hearted little fellows to try to find excuses for the young blackguards. So I think that after all, I won't complain to their parents. I'll leave it to you to point out the error of their ways to them. Mind you, I'm letting them off for your sakes not theirs. I'm more grateful to you than I can say for finding my cigarette-case. But you'll promise to give these boys a good straight talking to, won't you?"

In earnest guttural tones and shrill falsetto they promised.

"And in a way, of course, it's all to the good," said Mr. Newgate. "The sitting-room needed redecorating. I've been putting it off for years. This has forced my hand and it badly needed forcing. And, after all, a tulip bulb is only a tulip bulb."

"And a stew's only a stew," said William.

"Exactly . . . Well, I've enjoyed our little talk and I'm sure that your example will be a real help to those ill-conducted boys who came to my house . . . I'm afraid I shan't be able to recognise you when we next meet. I see very indistinctly without my glasses, but perhaps you'll introduce yourselves to me when and if we meet again will you?"

William made a growl of assent and Ginger a falsetto chirrup. Mr. Newgate rose from the seat.

"I must be getting on now. Don't bother to see me

home. I can find my way quite well. There's not far to go. Good-bye, my boys, and I'm *most* grateful to you."

They stood watching him till he vanished into the mist.

"That was a bit of luck," said Ginger as they began to walk back along the road.

"Yes," agreed William. He drew a deep breath. "Thank goodness it's all over an' we can get back to ordin'ry life again."

They walked on in silence for some time.

"About Lion Heart . . ." said Ginger at last.

"Yes?"

"Won't he feel a bit lonely in a big bowl when he's been used to that little one?"

"We could get him some friends . . . tiddlers . . ."

"An' newts."

"Yes . . . an' a stickleback if we could find one."

"An' tadpoles."

"We don't want *too* much of a crowd."

"We could do without the stickleback. I think they're a bit savage . . . Or——"

"Yes . . . Or——"

"What?"

"You could swop him for one of Frankie Parson's dormice. He's got two an' he wants to swop one for something else."

"We could think about it," said Ginger.

"Yes, we'll think about it," said William.

They parted at the gate of William's home. Mr. and Mrs. Brown were in the sitting-room when he entered it.

"Extraordinary!" Mrs. Brown was saying. "Ringing up one minute to say that he was coming to see you at once on an important matter, then ringing up almost immediately afterwards to say that it was a matter of no importance and he wasn't coming . . . Oh, William, where *have* you been? It's long past your bedtime." She sighed. "I shan't be sorry when my own bedtime comes. I've had a long and tiring day."

William considered.

"Yes," he said at last as if making an interesting discovery, "that's the sort of one I've had, too."

Chapter 7

William the Pot-holer

"He stayed down in this cave under the earth for four months," said William.

"Who did?" said Ginger.

"This man," said William, "an' he got six hundred pounds for it."

"Six hundred *pounds*!" said Ginger. "Gosh!"

"Yes, I can't think why everyone doesn't do it," said William. "If everyone stayed down in caves under the earth for four months an' got six hundred pounds, there wouldn't be any need for anyone to do any work at all. Sounds a jolly easy way of gettin' money. I can't think why everyone in the whole *world* doesn't do it."

"I don't b'lieve it'd turn out as easy as that," said Henry thoughtfully.

"It's worth tryin', anyway," said William. "I don't see why we shouldn't have a shot at it. It was in a newspaper, so it must be true."

"We'd get a bit bored in a cave for four months," said Douglas. "There wouldn't be anythin' to do."

"What did this man do?" said Ginger.

"He read . . ."

"What could we read?" said Douglas. "We've read all the books we've got."

"I've got a book my aunt gave me that I've never read, called *Heroes of Hebrew History*," said William. "We could take that."

"What else could we do?" said Douglas. "There wouldn't be room to play games."

"We could think," said William.

"What about?"

"Well . . . jus' anythin'. We needn't think about anythin' in particular. We could jus' think."

"Sounds jolly dull to me," said Douglas. "Jus' readin' *Heroes of Hebrew Hist'ry* an' thinkin' about nothin'."

"Then there's food," said Henry. "What did he do about food?"

"He took food down with him," said William.

"Gosh! It'd take more than a cave to hold the food *I'd* want in four months," said Douglas.

"I don't think we'd better stay down four whole months," said Henry. "It'd take us right into the middle of next term."

"An' I'd miss my birthday," said Douglas.

"Well, we could do less than four months an' take a bit less money," said William. "How much a day does it come to, Henry?"

"I'll have to work it out," said Henry, taking a pencil and notebook from his pocket and retiring to a corner of the old barn.

"Our parents'll wonder what's happened to us," said Ginger.

"We can leave notes for them, tellin' them we'll be back in four months with six hundred pounds," said William. "They can't grumble at us for earnin' six hundred pounds. It's only the same as the child workers in the old days 'cept that they worked in mills an' we're goin' to work in a cave.''

"Not much work," said Douglas with an ironic sniff. "Jus' readin' *Heroes of Hebrew Hist'ry* an' thinkin' about nothin' an' starvin' to death.''

"All right. Don't come if you don't want to," said William.

"It's about four pounds a day," said Henry.

"*Gosh!*" said William. "If we only did it for one month we'd have nearly enough money to last us for the rest of our lives.''

"Depends how long we lived," said Henry judicially.

"An' we've got to find a cave first," said Ginger. "We can't do anythin' without a cave.''

"What about the old quarry?" said Douglas.

"There aren't any really *deep* caves there," said William. "Not caves that go under the earth. There's lots of caves up the sides but there's no caves goin' deep into the earth. We've got to find a cave goin' deep into the earth same as this man had.''

"I once met a man that did pot-holin'," said Henry.

"What's that?" said William.

"They climb in an' out of holes at peril of their lives," said Henry.

"Sounds pretty good," said William with the interest that any fresh activity roused in him.

"But it's a *cave* we want," said Henry.

"Yes, of course," agreed William, dismissing potholes with reluctance. He was silent for a moment or two, then, "*Tell* you what!"

"Yes?"

"You know that wood at the bottom of Sir Gerald Markham's garden at Marleigh?"

"Yes."

"Well, in the war he had an air raid shelter built in the wood for men that happened to be workin' in the fields near, if a bomb came, an' it's still there. It goes right deep into the earth. We could use that."

"It doesn't b'long to us," said Douglas.

"Well, he wouldn't mind," said William. "Not Sir Gerald. He never minds us goin' into his woods."

"An' anyway he's in America so he wouldn't know," said Ginger.

"Well, that's what we'll do then," said William. "We'll use this air raid shelter an' it'll count same as a cave."

"I've jus' thought of somethin'," said Ginger.

"What?"

'Who's goin' to give us this money?"

A silence fell.

"Well, *someone* must," said William. "This man in the newspaper got it so *someone* must have given it him."

"I think the man the cave belonged to gave it him," said Henry.

"Then I s'pose Sir Gerald'll give it us," said William with a suggestion of doubt in his voice.

"I s'pose he might," said Henry with more than a suggestion of doubt in his voice.

"Anyway, we'll go an' have a look at it an' fix up when to start," said William. "Let's meet there first thing tomorrow mornin'."

William arrived first at the stretch of woodland that ran across the end of Sir Gerald's ground and formed part of his estate. It took him a long time to discover the ancient air raid shelter and a still longer time to discover the entrance to it. The whole thing was overgrown with brambles, ivy and coarse weeds. The others arrived shortly after he had discovered the entrance and joined him in

A SHORT FLIGHT OF RICKETY STEPS LED DOWN INTO A DANK,
DARK PIT.

the work of clearing a passage through the undergrowth
and revealing a short flight of rickety steps that led down
into a dank, dark pit.

"We couldn't stay down there for four months,
William," said Henry.

"We couldn't stay down for four days," said Douglas.

Even Ginger shook his head slowly.

"We'd better give it up, William," he said.

But William, having decided on a plan of action, could
not easily be persuaded to abandon it.

" 'Course we won't give it up," he said. "We've set out
to do it an' we're *going* to do it." He peered through the

thick undergrowth. "It only needs a bit of fixin' up, that's all it needs. Come on!"

Pushing aside a curtain of ivy and detaching himself from a strongly entrenched bramble that grew by the entrance, he set his feet on the rickety steps, which promptly gave way beneath him and flung him headlong into the 'cave'. The others followed more cautiously. William scrambled to his feet, wiped his eyes clear of the shower of earth that had fallen on him and inspected his surroundings.

The roof was of galvanised iron supported by sagging wooden stakes, the walls were of crumbling earth and their feet sank into a morass of mud and slime.

"It's awful, William," said Ginger.

"It's not," said William. "I *told* you. It only needs a bit of fixin' up. 'Course it's a bit damp. It was rainin' last night, wasn't it? Any place'd be a bit damp after it'd been raining all night. Well, it's news to *me* if places aren't a bit damp after it's been raining all night. It only needs fixin' up."

"Well how'll we fix it up?" said Henry. "It looks past fixin' up to me. The walls are fallin' in an' the roof's fallin' down."

William threw a critical glance around him.

"We jus' want a few pieces of wood an' stuff to prop it up with," he said. "Looks like a prehistoric cave. We could do some paintin's on the walls an' turn it into a prehistoric cave."

"No, we couldn't," said Henry, " 'cause everyone knows it's an air raid shelter."

"Oh, all right," said William. "Well, let's find some stuff to prop it up with. There's bound to be bits of wood in a wood. We might find some blown down branches that'd do. Let's have a look, anyway."

They climbed out of the shelter and fought their way through the undergrowth, picking up any pieces of wood they could find and pulling at any branch low enough for them to reach.

"Doesn't seem much good," said Ginger at last. "The ones on the ground are too small and the big ones won't come off the trees."

William had wandered to the side of the wood.

'Look!" he said.

A field ran alongside of the wood, separated from it by a hedge. In the middle of the field was a caravan and, at the end of the field, behind the caravan, the ground rose sharply up to a row of newly erected council houses, bricks and paintwork gleamingly fresh from the builders' hands. An ancient horse cropped the grass nearby. There were no signs of human habitation.

"*Look!*" said William again as the others joined him.

His eyes were fixed on a pile of scrap metal that sprawled at the back of the caravan—sheets of galvanised iron, buckets, a fender, a fireguard, tools of various kinds, all broken and rusty.

"They'd do to prop up the walls," said William.

"But they're not ours," objected Douglas.

"Well, they're only rubbish," said William. "No one could want them. Look at them, jus' lyin' about, gettin' rustier an' rustier. We'd be doin' *good* takin' them away. An' anyway, we'd only *borrow* them. We'd take 'em back at the end of four months. I bet no one'd miss 'em. Come on!"

He was already wriggling through a convenient gap in the hedge. The others followed.

The ancient horse raised its head and looked at them inquiringly.

"Good ole horse!" said William.

As if reassured, the horse returned to cropping grass.

"Let's get 'em quick," said William, "before anyone comes."

They moved the metal sheets from the field to the wood, pushing them through the hole in the hedge, easing them with difficulty down into the 'cave' and placing them against the sides and on the ground. The pieces they placed against the sides showed a strong tendency to collapse, and the ones on the ground showed an equally strong tendency to rise up and hit them in the face whenever they tried to walk on them.

"Let's get the fender and the fire-guard," said William. "They'll help to keep it up."

Fender and fire-guard were fetched and placed precariously against the iron sheets that lined the walls.

"It's jolly good," said William. "At least it will be when they sort of settle down . . . Now let's clear away all that stuff that's growing over the doorway. We don't want to die of suffocation before the four months are up. Let's fetch those shears an' spades an' things."

They fetched the various tools from behind the caravan, and, working strenuously and in (comparative) silence, hacked away at the forest of ivy, brambles and coarse weeds.

"Let's get those buckets, too," panted William at last. "We can use them to stand on to cut those bits of trees that come down too low. They've nearly strangled me already."

Douglas fetched the two buckets, and William and Ginger climbed on to them, cutting down the lower twigs of the surrounding trees till both buckets collapsed throwing the boys into a rank growth of nettles. Their yells of pain occupied the next few moments, then William returned to an inspection of his 'cave'. The ivy, brambles and twigs that they had cut down now completely blocked the entrance.

"There was a rake," said William. "Fetch the rake, Douglas, so's we can push the stuff away."

Douglas returned to the caravan and brought back the rake.

"It's the last thing left," he said. "We've got it all now."

"Oh . . ." said William. For the first time a dim compunction stirred at his heart. "I wonder—I wonder if it belonged to anyone in particular. We—*we mus'* have left some of it."

"No, we haven't," said Douglas. "We've taken it all."

"Let's go'n' have a look," said William.

The four presented a strange spectacle—their faces and clothing heavily stained with earth and lichen, their hair festooned with ivy, bramble and twigs.

They made their way through the hedge and stood behind the caravan looking around them. Where the old iron had been was a stretch of yellowing beaten-down grass and a small weed-infested border.

"We've *stolen* it," said Douglas with a note of gloomy satisfaction in his voice. "I *said* it wasn't ours."

'Well, we can't bring it back," said William. "We could only jus' get it down there, we'd never get it up."

"There's nothin' we *can* do," said Ginger.

"We could pay for it," said Henry uncertainly.

"We haven't any money," said William. He was silent for a few moments then suddenly he brightened. "*Tell* you what!"

"Yes?"

"We could sort of pay for it by tidyin' up a bit," he said. "We could cut all that long grass an' take out the weeds an' sort of straighten it up. People are gen'rally jolly pleased when someone does a bit of gard'nin' for

them. It gen'rally puts them in a good temper, 'specially
if you don't pull up the wrong things . . . Let's try it
anyway. Let's get the shears an' fork an' have a go at it."

They fetched shears and fork and set to work . . . cutting the long yellow grass, taking up the weeds from the
little flower-bed, forking over the soil and revealing a few
still sturdy clumps of thrift and houseleeks.

The old horse joined them and stood watching with
apparent interest.

"Good ole horse!" said William and the horse gave a
little whinny as if in answer.

"Well, we've made it look a bit better," said Henry,
standing back to survey their work. "Let's take all that
cut grass an' stuff into the wood out of the way."

They carried the cut grass by armfuls into the wood
then returned to give the place a final inspection.

"Yes, it cert'nly looks diff'rent from what it did," said
William.

"That may be the trouble," said Douglas darkly.

The horse put down its head and nuzzled William's
shoulder in a friendly fashion.

"Seems to like me," said William sheepishly. He
stroked the silky nose. "Good ole horse!"

"We'd better be goin'," said Douglas, throwing an
apprehensive glance around.

But William's whole attention was now given to his new
friend.

"Wonder if he'd let me get on his back," he said.
"Gosh! I wish I'd lived in the days when knights went into
battle on a horse. I'd like to've been a knight goin' into
battle on a horse . . . I'm goin' to pretend to be one. You
be my squire, Ginger, an' Henry an' Douglas the foot
soldiers." He raised his voice to a loud imperious note.
"Saddle my steed, Squire Ginger, and we'll to battle."

"Where's the saddle?" said Ginger.

William slipped off his blazer and gave it to Ginger. Ginger spread it over the horse's back.

"I'm goin' to try to get up on him," said William. "I—" he stopped suddenly.

An old man was entering the gate that led from the road to the field. The horse gave a whinny of welcome and trotted down to meet him.

"Let's go quick," said Douglas.

"We can't," said William. "He's got my blazer. Mother'd be mad with me if I went home without it. She was mad with me yesterday 'cause I borrowed her potato peeler to try 'n' mend my diesel engine an' forgot to take it back."

"Did it mend your diesel engine?"

"No, an' she couldn't mend the potato peeler."

They walked slowly down to the gate, where the old man stood patting the horse's neck. He had a pleasant weather-beaten face and bright blue eyes. He turned to the boys with a kindly smile.

" 'E's allus got a greetin' for me when I comes 'ome," he said.

William blinked.

"Is it . . . ?" he began.

"Do you . . . ?" began Ginger.

"Is that your home?" said Henry, pointing to the caravan.

The old man's smile died away.

"Yes," he said. "The only 'ome I've got an' they want to take it from me."

"Who does?" said William.

"The council," said the old man. "The blinkin' council. They says they've 'ad a complaint an' they wants to turn me out. It's Sir Gerald's land an' 'e give me permission

**"'E'S ALLUS GOT A GREETIN' FOR ME WHEN I COMES 'OME,"
HE SAID.**

to live 'ere an' this is 'is old 'orse that I looks after.
Pegasus, 'is name is, but I calls 'im Peg. But they says
that makes no difference. Little Lords o' Creation, they
are, an' all! They say they can turn me out over Sir
Gerald's head an' put me in an Old People's 'Ome.''

"Gosh!" said William indignantly, "but they *can't*."

"Seems they can," said the old man sadly. "Seems
they've got the lor on their side . . . I couldn't *breathe* in
an Old People's 'Ome, away from me caravan an' me old
'orse. I've lived with 'orses all me life. In the Royal 'Orse
Artillery, I was, in the first war. I've allus 'ad to do with

'em. An' I'm not no trouble to no one. I keeps me place clean. I wash me own clothes an' I cooks me own food an' I've never been beholden to no one not in all me life . . . But they've 'ad a complaint an' they're goin' to turn me out."

"What sort of a complaint?" said Henry.

"Somethin' to do with old iron."

"Old iron?" said William.

"Yes . . . A cousin o' mine what deals in it came an' left me a load of the stuff a month or so ago. 'E'd got more than 'is cart could manage an' 'e asks me to 'old on to it, as it were, but I've 'eard nothin' since an' I can't get rid of it 'cause I said I'd keep it for 'im an' 'e might turn up any day, so there it is, an' she's made a complaint an' they're comin' along this afternoon, pokin' an' pryin'." He turned and looked down the road. Two women stood at the crossroads, talking. "That's them, I shouldn't be surprised. Look at 'em, natterin' away. Plottin' an' plannin', little Lords o' Creation!"

"Listen," said William urgently. "We've got somethin' to tell you."

One of the two women who stood talking at the crossroads was tall and thin and sharp-looking. Everything about her was sharp and thin. Her nose was sharp and thin and, when she spoke, her voice was sharp and thin. Even the glances she threw at the surrounding countryside were sharp and thin as if suspecting the trees and hedges of indulging in unlawful activities.

"Really, Mrs. Galloway!" she was saying. "It's too tiresome. I can't think why Mrs. Medlar isn't here. She asked us to meet her at the bus stop at eleven thirty, didn't she?"

"Yes," said the other woman. She was large and shapeless and loosely put together. Her face was empty except for the usual features, and an air of weary aristocracy hung about her. She had been elected to the council solely because her grandfather had presented Hadley with its swimming baths and recreation ground, and she could generally be relied on to assent to any proposal that was put to her. "Or did she say twelve thirty? Time goes so quickly."

"I hope she won't keep us waiting much longer," said Miss Beedale. "I have every minute of every day carefully planned, and five minutes lost throws me out for the whole day, if not the week . . . Of course, I'm glad she made the complaint. It gives us a handle. Otherwise we might not have been able to turn the old man out. Really, these wretched old people shouldn't be allowed to plonk themselves down wherever they've a mind to. They should be shut away in old people's homes where they can't make nuisances of themselves, or where they can be firmly dealt with if they do . . . Ah, here's another bus. She may be on this one."

The bus drew up and a stumpy little woman, carrying a heavily laden shopping-bag, descended from it. The short skirt revealed a pair of massive legs, and she waddled towards the two other women on high-heeled shoes that were obviously too small for the plump little feet. The hat—above the scowling brows—was a top-heavy erection of clustered flowers and an open coat displayed a tight purple jumper with strand upon strand of iridescent beads. Her face was set in lines of ill-humour.

"You're late, Mrs. Medlar," said Miss Beedale.

"Bin doin' me bits of shoppin' down in 'Adley," said Mrs. Medlar. "Disgraceful, the way they keep you 'angin' round in them shops. Saucy lazy minxes servin' in all of 'em! I told one of 'em what I thought of 'er an' all I got back was a lot of sauce."

"Yes, yes," said Miss Beedale impatiently. "Well, I

think the matter was fully explained to you in the letter you received. My name is Miss Beedale and this is Mrs. Galloway." Mrs. Galloway inclined her head graciously in Mrs. Medlar's direction. "We have come to investigate your complaint. We represent the council and the council have agreed to abide by our decision . . . So let us waste no more time . . . The caravan you complain of is in the next field, I believe."

The three began to walk along the road.

"Junk!" said Mrs. Medlar. "Junk an' old iron all over the place! Slum, that's what it is. Nothin' more nor less. Well, I've not rose up in the world to 'ave to look at junk an' old iron out of me winder. Might as well 'ave stayed in Poplar. Classy neighbourhood, this 'ere's supposed to be. Not much class in junk an' old iron. Disgustin', I calls it. Disgustin'!"

"Yes, yes, Mrs. Medlar," said Miss Beedale. "We'll do all we can for you."

They had reached the gate where the old man, the four boys and the horse were standing. Mrs. Galloway inclined her head graciously in their direction. Mrs. Medlar threw them a black look. Pegasus uttered a derisive whinny. Henry opened the gate and the three women entered. Inside the field they stood for a few moments, looking at the caravan.

"I must say it looks tidy enough," said Miss Beedale. There was disappointment in her voice.

"Wait till you sees the back," snarled Mrs. Medlar. "Junk an' old iron! Makes me sick to look at it."

"Come along then," said Miss Beedale. "Let us waste no more time. Let us go round to the back."

They walked round to the back of the caravan. The boys had done their work well. The grass was neatly cut, the little flower border, though deficient in flowers, was

freshly dug over. There were no signs of neglect anywhere.

Mrs. Medlar stood looking at it, breathing heavily, her
face suffused with purple, her mouth opening and shutting
soundlessly.

"Really, Mrs. Medlar!" said Miss Beedale. "You've
brought us here on a fool's errand, the place is in perfect
order. There are no possible grounds for complaint, and
certainly no grounds for action . . . Really, as if we hadn't
enough work on our hands without being brought out
here on a wild-goose chase!" She turned to Mrs. Galloway. "Come along. Let us go back to Hadley and waste
no more time."

"But listen!" shrilled Mrs. Medlar. "I take my dying
oath it was there. Junk! Muck! . . ."

"Good-bye, Mrs. Medlar," said Miss Beedale coldly.

She gave a curt nod to the old man, threw a suspicious
glance at the boys, a quelling glance at Pegasus and set
off at a brisk pace across the field, accompanied by Mrs.
Galloway, who paused only to bow graciously to the
group at the gate as she passed it.

"Listen!" screamed Mrs. Medlar. "*Listen!*"

She went to the gate and waddled after them, her voice
raised in shrill remonstrance.

The old man and the boys stood watching them. Pegasus's whinny seemed to hold a note of sardonic amusement.

The old man chuckled.

"Well, I don't think we'll see the little Lords o' Creation
back 'ere for a bit," he said, "thanks to you nippers. You
did me a good turn an' no mistake."

"You don't want the stuff back, do you?" said William.

"No, no. Leave it where it is. If me cousin comes along
I'll tell 'im how to get to it. No one goes anear of that

"REALLY, MRS. MEDLAR!" SAID MISS BEEDALE. "YOU'VE
BROUGHT US HERE ON A FOOL'S ERRAND!"